CHAPTER ONE

Today my husband is getting married. The words thundered in Lauren's head as she raced towards the line of parked cars, aware that a dark green Range Rover, hurtling through the gate behind her, was heading in the same direction.

With a deft twist of the steering wheel, she swung her Mini straight into the one remaining gap in the hospital car park. Gravel spurted out from under her tyres, rattling onto the bonnet of the Range Rover, as she slammed on the brakes.

Snatching her bag from the seat, Lauren threw open the door and leaped out, locking it behind her. Glancing up, she saw blue eyes blaze down at her, but it wasn't their anger that sent shock waves radiating throughout her body. It was the face.

A face exactly like Rick's. And yet—not quite the same.

The good looks were similar, in a rather angular sort of way. But the dark hair that curled slightly over well-shaped ears was definitely in need of a trim. Rick's was never like that. He was fastidious about his appearance. Obsessively so. And this man's eyes were wider set, and a deeper blue.

Today my husband is getting married.

1

Ex-husband, Lauren told herself fiercely. Would Rick never be out of her mind? Was that why any man looked like him?

But this one resembled him so much. *And he's probably exactly the same type,* she thought. *Overwhelming. Overpowering. And oversexed.*

The last word hovered in her brain. *Definitely the same type,* she decided.

With no time for apologies, she turned and ran towards the main door of the hospital complex. The wall clock showed it was two minutes to eight as she rushed into a foyer seething with people, and jumped into a waiting lift, squashing herself against the nearest corner.

Its doors were sighing to a close, when two hands appeared on either side, holding them apart. Square shoulders in a charcoal-grey suit eased themselves past. As the rest of his lean frame followed through the narrow opening, Lauren recognised the driver of the Range Rover. And she could see, from the taut thrust of his jaw, that his annoyance hadn't faded.

Lauren inched sideways along the lift wall, behind two chatting auxiliaries, hoping he wouldn't notice her. But at the movement his head swung round and she found herself spiked on the ice of his gaze.

'Do you make a habit of cutting up other drivers like that?'

His voice was low and deep, the vowels extended in a way Lauren felt she should

2

ALL I WANT FOR CHRISTMAS

Julie Coffin

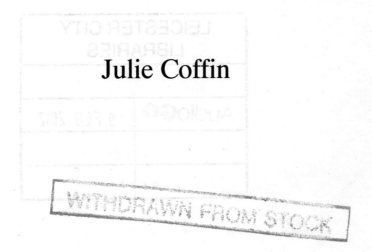
CHIVERS

British Library Cataloguing in Publication Data available

This Large Print edition published by AudioGo Ltd, Bath, 2011.
Published by arrangement with the Author.

U.K. Hardcover ISBN 978 1 445 83764 2
U.K. Softcover ISBN 978 1 445 83765 9

Printed and bound in Great Britain by
MPG Books Group Limited

recognise. A pleasant voice, but each word was spoken in a tone that speared through her.

Conversation ceased abruptly as the other lift occupants swivelled round to stare. Lauren felt colour burn up her neck into her cheeks.

Her chin jutted.

'You were racing me for that space and, as I was there first, it was rightly mine.' Somehow her voice sounded petulant.

'You evidently failed to notice in your haste,' he grated, 'that it's a staff-only car park.'

Lauren lifted her head, wishing she wasn't five foot three and half-hidden behind other people. Even by standing on tiptoe and peering over their shoulders, it was difficult to look him straight in the eye.

'I am a member of staff.'

'From when?' His voice held disbelief.

'Today.'

The lift doors opened while she spoke and everyone surged forward. He stood back to let her step out, but she shook her head and pressed the button for the second floor. Apart from the two of them, the lift was empty now, moving silently upwards.

He was quite a bit taller than Rick, Lauren noticed, still unable to avoid the comparison. Thinner, though. Some men grow paunchy in their mid-thirties. Reaching that stage had upset Rick so much. But there was not a spare ounce on this man. He was almost too thin.

3

And yet they were incredibly alike.

Are women always attracted to the same type of man? she wondered, and quickly retracted the thought. *What a stupid thing to think. As if I could ever be attracted to any man, after three years with Rick.*

And today he's getting married again.

The memory caught her unexpectedly. Unable to prevent it, her chin quivered and she pressed her lips tightly together, her eyes brimming.

'Are you all right?'

There was a softer note to the man's voice now. Looking up, Lauren saw the frost had melted from his eyes, leaving them full of compassion.

But why? she asked herself. Surely the pain that sliced into her whenever she thought of Rick's rejection wasn't apparent? She prided herself on keeping it under control. Letting no-one know the anguish of her rejection.

So why did she have to meet a man like him, today of all days?

'Quite all right, thank you,' she replied tersely, as with blurred eyes she stepped swiftly out of the lift when the doors opened again. She heard them close and the car travel on up to the next floor.

The crèche was at the far end of the corridor. She'd had her interview there. A long room with tall windows, full of light, the walls covered with collages and paintings created by

4

the children.

Lauren keyed in the door code.

'Hi, I'm Sarah Walsh.'

The greeting came from a girl who looked up from where she was sitting, slicing a roll of wallpaper into squares.

'Great for the kids' paintings,' she explained, putting down the roll and holding out her hand. 'You must be Lauren Mallory, the new crèche manager? You're obviously not one of the mums. No lively little attachment. Come on into the kitchen and grab a cup of coffee.'

Rising to her feet, she led the way into an adjoining room. 'Kettle's just boiled. You won't get much chance, once the kids arrive.'

Taking a jar from a high shelf, she spooned granules into a mug patterned with black cats.

'We bought this last Christmas for Cathy, your predecessor. She thought it was because of her name—until I let out it was meant to represent her!'

'Lucky, you mean?' Lauren asked.

Sarah chuckled. 'No—catty!' Then her face sobered. 'Perhaps I shouldn't say that to her replacement. Anyway, we weren't sorry to see her go. Sugar?' She unsnapped the lid of a plastic box.

'No, thanks,' Lauren replied, taking the mug and perching herself on the corner of the table. 'I hope you won't feel the same about me.'

'And so say all of us!' the other girl replied, laughing as she picked up a carton of milk. 'There's been a lot of speculation about what you'll be like.' She tugged at the top of the container. 'Oh, now it's gone everywhere!'

Soaking up the spilt milk with a paper towel, she continued. 'One or two noses were put out of joint when we heard we were getting an outsider.'

'Outsider?' Lauren queried.

'Not one of us,' Sarah explained. 'You must have been told there are six staff working in the crèche. Three full and three part-timers. Well, everyone thought one of the full-timers would get the job when Cathy left.'

'That sounds ominous.'

Sarah dropped the wet paper towel into a bin. 'You may get some hassle from one who shall be nameless. I'll just say that she does have the longest nose for putting out of joint!'

'Thanks for the warning,' Lauren said. 'And while we're on our own, how about giving me a few pointers about how the crèche is run?'

Sarah gave her a surprised look. 'That's for you to decide, isn't it?'

'Well, I have a few ideas of my own to bring in gradually, but small children don't like their routine being changed.'

'Weren't you told anything at your interview?'

Lauren finished her coffee, rinsed the mug and picked up a cloth.

'Not a great deal. Everyone had gone home, and Miss Knolls—Cathy—showed me round. I'd have preferred to see the children.' She smiled as she put the mug back on the shelf. 'I'm sure you can give me a far better idea.'

'Well, like I said, there's the six of us. Full-timers—Helen, Emma and Jane. Part-timers—me, Gina and Lucy. The children belong to hospital staff and can only be here when that person's on duty.' Sarah wrinkled her nose. 'Although that does get stretched a bit sometimes.'

'How do you mean?'

'A few of the staff who do a split duty—a morning and an evening—often bring the child at eight-thirty when we open, leave it with us all day, and a husband or partner collects it again at six when we close. It gives them a quiet hour or two to sleep, or go shopping, or whatever.'

'But it shouldn't happen,' Lauren pointed out.

Sarah shrugged. 'How would you feel, coping with a crying baby or lively toddler, knowing you had another hectic shift to face, with no rest?'

Lauren smiled ruefully. 'I see. How do you deal with problem children?'

Laughing, Sarah said, 'It's only when they get home they're a problem. There's far too much going on here for them to be unhappy.'

'Some must be,' Lauren insisted.

7

'Well, there is one,' Sarah replied slowly. 'Zoe. A four-year-old. Only been here a few days. At that age, they can take a while to settle.' She chuckled. 'The babies are best. Far easier. And they grow up completely used to us. We really miss some of them when they start school.'

'So what's the routine when there's a new admission?' Lauren persisted.

Rinsing her hands under the tap, Sarah dried them on a paper towel. 'We ask the mums for any special details. Whether they have a toy or comforter of some kind when they have their sleep. Likes and dislikes with food. I'm sure you know the sort of thing.'

She turned as the door opened and two older women came in. One of them frowned on seeing Lauren. Lauren couldn't prevent her gaze from straying to the woman's nose, remembering Sarah's earlier words.

'Helen and Jane.' Sarah introduced them. 'This is Lauren Mallory.'

'And what are we supposed to call you?' Helen demanded, unbuttoning her jacket.

Late forties, Lauren judged, studying the short greying hair that fringed a narrow, prematurely lined face. Probably resenting a twenty-five-year-old taking over.

She smiled. 'By my first name, of course. Isn't that what you all do?'

'Catherine Knolls was always called Ms Knolls.'

8

'And Catty behind her back,' Sarah added with a wide grin.

Helen swung round, glaring furiously at the younger girl. 'It's about time you learned to show some respect for senior staff. I wouldn't be surprised if it was because of you and your flippant remarks that Cathy left.'

'Of course it wasn't,' Sarah protested, her cheeks bright with colour.

Three more girls came in, hesitating when they saw Lauren.

'You must be Emma, Gina and Lucy. I'm Lauren.'

At her friendly greeting, they relaxed, and started chattering again as they quickly made themselves mugs of coffee.

'Look, being completely inexperienced here,' Lauren said, joining them, 'I'm going to need all the help and advice you can give me.'

'Inexperienced?' Helen swiftly picked up on the word. 'Do you mean you've never worked in a hospital crèche before?'

'Not a hospital crèche,' Lauren replied. 'I originally worked as a nanny.'

'A nanny!' Helen snapped. 'There's quite a difference from working for a privileged family to a crèche like this. Our children's parents range from cleaners to consultants.'Coffee granules scattered as her hand shook. 'But I suppose you must have formal qualifications or you wouldn't be here.'

'Helen!' Sarah protested. 'That's the sort of

9

remark you'd expect of me!'

'It's all right, Sarah,' Lauren interrupted. 'Helen has every right to ask.' She turned to the older woman. 'Before I worked as a nanny, I obtained a Diploma in Childcare and Education, as I'm sure you did, Helen.'

'Of course,' Helen answered sharply, 'but practical experience has far greater importance than anything on paper.'

'I couldn't agree more,' Lauren replied quietly. 'Which is why I want to widen my experience.' She glanced at her watch. 'Now, shouldn't we be getting ready? The children will be arriving any minute, won't they?'

Helen's long nose twitched. 'Oh, you don't have to worry about anything, Ms Mallory. After we close each night, some of us make sure everything's prepared for the next morning. Keeping the children happy and contented is our main concern. I suppose, being a nanny, things were done differently.'

'I said I *originally* worked as a nanny, Helen.' Lauren, remembering the reason for her change of job to this one, paused before continuing. 'More recently I was working for a pharmaceutical company. The crèche there catered for over fifty children under five, rising to seventy or more during school holidays, when brothers and sisters joined them.'

'Well, you couldn't have had any real contact with such a large number,' Helen retorted.

'Oh, but we did, Helen. Each member of staff was responsible for only three infants. We knew, and loved, each child as our own. Now,' Lauren said briskly. 'I think it's time we finished this coffee and started some work.'

*   *   *

The morning progressed rapidly. All the children began to arrive at the same time and the room filled with noise. Voices shrieked. Laughter bubbled. Feet clattered. Chairs scraped. Cupboard doors crashed open.

And every single child is happy, Lauren observed, watching them. But even as she thought that, the door opened again.

Through it came a weary-looking woman, pregnant with what Lauren decided from her size could only be twins or triplets. And entangled in her long black coat, tiny fingers gripping it tightly, was a child.

With head hidden by a hood and face buried into the coat, Lauren couldn't work out whether it was a boy or girl. What she could see was that the child was deeply distressed.

'Now then, Zoe. We don't want all that fuss, do we?' Helen was marching over, one hand outstretched towards the child's shoulder.

'It's all right, Helen,' Lauren said, quickly stepping forward. 'You carry on with the face-painting. There's quite a queue growing.'

She sat on her heels beside the sobbing

11

child. 'Hullo, Zoe. I'm Lauren.' The child's fingers twisted themselves more deeply into the black coat.

'Oh, come on, Zoe, you know I've got to go,' the woman murmured, desperately trying to release the clinging hands.

'Zoe,' Lauren said quietly. 'I'm new here today. Just like you were when you first came. Remember? And I don't know where anything is kept. Now I need to find the Lego. Could you could help me?'

The hood moved a little as the head inside swivelled round. One bright red cheek appeared, part-hidden by a waterfall of straight dark hair.

'Sarah said it was in one of the cupboards,' Lauren continued, slowly standing up. 'But I can't find the right one.'

One by one, Zoe's fingers released their tight clasp of the coat, then pushed back the enveloping hood of her anorak, to reveal huge tear-wet brown eyes under a thick untidy fringe.

'I know where,' she announced firmly, catching hold of Lauren's hand and starting to run across the room.

'Her father will collect her at six,' the woman called, turning to leave.

'Okay!' Lauren called back.

As the day wore on, she began to wonder whether she'd said the right thing to Zoe. The child never left her side. By the end of the afternoon, taught by her self-appointed little instructor, Lauren knew every child's name and whether they were horrible or nice.

'You're working wonders, Lauren, All Zoe's ever done before is cry,' Sarah commented, tucking one of the babies into a buggy, ready for collection. 'She's only been here a week. It just shows she's been taking in everything, though. Quite a bright little thing, isn't she?'

Children had come and gone during the day, as their mothers came on or went off duty. By six o'clock there were only half-a-dozen left. Sarah and the other girls had them dressed in outdoor clothes, waiting. Those who were big enough helped. Others gathered up paintings and things they'd constructed to take home.

By six-fifteen the room was empty of children—except for one. Zoe. Lauren looked at her watch. Helen was clearing up and preparing everything for the following morning. The other staff had already left.

Zoe stood beside Lauren, gazing anxiously up at her every now and then. 'Don't go.' The small voice was urgent.

Lauren bent down. 'Of course I won't go, sweetheart. There's no need to worry. Your Daddy will be here soon. Mummy said he'd collect you.'

'Mummy's gone.'

'Only to work, sweetheart,' Lauren explained.

Zoe shook her head, sending her dark hair swirling round her face. 'No! Gone! Gone! Gone!' The words rose into a shriek.

Lauren's hands caught the child's in her own. What an insecure little creature she was. What on earth could have made her like this?

'Of course your Mummy's not gone, poppet. She'll be at home right now. Making your tea, I expect. What do you think it will be?'

Brown eyes gazed solemnly up at her. 'No, Daddy makes our tea.' *Good for him,* Zoe thought. *But I wish he'd collect his daughter.*

'That's everything, Ms Mallory.' Helen appeared, buttoning her jacket.

'Are you all right to stay on with Zoe? Dr Trevissick's probably caught up in some emergency. He really has no idea of time.'

It was six-thirty now. *This really is a bit much,* Lauren fumed, studying Zoe who sat, perched on a chair beside her, white-faced and anxious.

'Has my Daddy gone away, too?'

'No, sweetheart, I'm sure he'll be here very soon,' Lauren soothed.

Didn't her father realise how important it is to a child to be there when expected? Knowing how difficult it was for Zoe to settle into the crèche, surely he must know that this sort of behaviour would only make her more insecure. *If Dr Trevissick isn't here in five minutes, I'll have him paged, whatever he's doing,* she raged.

'Daddy's not coming.' A tear brimmed over

14

and slid down the tired little face, followed by another and another.

'He will be here soon, Zoe. I expect he's busy making someone better.' The little girl slowly shook her head.

'My Mummy didn't come back,' she wept, and Lauren could feel the tears wet against her own cheek as she held the child close.

A myriad doubts were racing through her head. Why hadn't Zoe's mother collected her, if she knew her husband was likely to be late? Was she one of those Sarah had spoken about—a nurse working a split shift?

Could she still be a nurse in that heavily pregnant state? It seemed doubtful. Lauren tried to remember whether the woman had been wearing a uniform under her coat. Perhaps she worked as a secretary or receptionist.

Six forty-five. *Okay, Dr Trevissick,* she thought grimly, *if you haven't a home to go to, I have.* Picking up the telephone, she asked for him to be paged, requesting that he come to the crèche immediately.

Minutes later, the door burst open. Trying not to disturb the now sleeping child she held in her arms, Lauren turned her head. Striding through the doorway, charcoal-grey jacket swirling round his narrow hips, was Rick's lookalike.

CHAPTER TWO

Dr Trevissick ignored Lauren, his gaze on the sleeping child she held. 'What's happened to Zoe?' he demanded.

'Nothing that a little loving care won't cure,' Lauren replied frostily. 'She's very distressed, waiting over an hour for you to collect her. You do realise, Dr Trevissick, that this crèche closes at six o'clock?'

He glanced down at his watch and his expression softened. 'I had no idea it was so late. I really am sorry. It's been one of those days, I'm afraid.'

Lauren saw the corners of his mouth tilt, and the sharp planes of his angular face relax into a smile.

'Could you hang onto Zoe for another five minutes, while I give the nursing staff instructions for a change of medication? I must do it before I leave tonight.' He caught the look on Lauren's face. 'I promise I won't be longer than ten at the most.'

Lauren sighed. She was so late already that another five minutes wasn't going to make much difference.

'Okay then. Five minutes—no longer.'

It was an enchanting smile, Lauren decided, after he'd gone. He certainly knew how to turn on the charm. Her mouth tightened. That was just what everyone had said about Rick.

Zoe was becoming a dead weight on her left arm, and as Lauren moved to ease it, the little girl's eyes flew open. 'Mummy!' For a second her small face was radiant, then the expression vanished.

'Daddy's taking you home to see her any minute now. He was here—he's just gone to speak to one of the nurses, then he'll be back.'

'Mummy doesn't live at our house.'

Lauren groaned inwardly. Why on earth hadn't she thought? Her mother and father were divorced, or separated, or something. Perhaps her mother had married again. That would explain the forthcoming baby, or babies. Zoe must have been staying with her mother over the weekend. That was why she'd brought her in this morning.

How stupid of her to think that everyone else led a happy family life, and that only hers was a disaster. It was so common nowadays. One in three marriages ended in divorce, isn't that what statistics said? *Why should it only be me? Every third person I meet is in the same boat. Or should that be every sixth?* she puzzled.

'So your Daddy's going to take you home and make tea, is he?' she asked, hoping to distract the little girl.

Zoe nodded. 'Fish fingers and chips. That's what we always have.'

'Every day?' Lauren questioned.

The child nodded again. 'We've got a

microwave. Is Daddy coming soon? I'm hungry.'

Lauren checked her watch. 'Very soon.' *And if he doesn't,* she thought, *there'll be ructions, and they won't be from Zoe.*

The door opened, cautiously this time, and Dr Trevissick came back in.

'You said five minutes—not fifteen.'

His apologetic smile made Lauren's anger melt.

'Oh, never mind. You'd better take Zoe home for her fish fingers and chips before she falls asleep again.'

He frowned. 'She'll be lucky if she gets that tonight. I've been working all weekend and . . .' He paused and raised one dark eyebrow at Lauren. 'I overslept, which made me extremely late arriving here this morning, so I haven't had a chance to get to the supermarket.'

'You do feed her properly, don't you?' Lauren questioned sharply.

'Of course!'

'So what are you giving her tonight?'

'There's a take-away on our route home.'

'A take-away! And how often does she have that kind of junk food?' Almost snatching the startled little girl from Lauren's arms, Dr Trevissick marched towards the door.

'How and what I feed my own daughter are—'

'In actual fact, while she's under my care, Dr Trevissick, how and what you feed your

18

daughter is my concern as well as yours,' Lauren interrupted, following them into the corridor and locking the door behind her. She ran to catch up as he strode out into the damp November night.

'Must you keep snapping at my heels like an angry terrier?' he grated.

'Then stop rushing off like that,' Lauren suggested. 'Bouncing Zoe about will make her sick.'

He stopped so unexpectedly that Lauren cannoned into him, and found one long arm wrapped around her waist, steadying her.

'Look, Miss Whoever-You-Are, will you please go away,' he said in a voice verging on anger. 'You've blighted my day from the moment I arrived. Now you're doing it again. Please remember Zoe is only in your charge from eight-thirty in the morning until six at night. Before and after that, I decide what she will do and how—be it eating, sleeping, or playing with her toys.'

With the strength of his arm preventing her from escaping, his face was so close that Lauren felt his every word warm her cheek, sending her heartbeat racing.

Overwhelming. Overpowering. So like Rick it was unbearable.

Wrenching herself away, she glowered up at him. Under the lights of the car park, a scattering of raindrops sparkled against the black swathe of his hair. Even his curving eyebrows glittered.

Today my husband is married again by now.
Looking at this man, how can I ever forget?

Bitterness filled her voice when she replied. 'You're quite right, Dr Trevissick. Zoe is only in my charge from eight-thirty in the morning until six at night. Before and after that, she is your responsibility.' Her voice rose. 'So please remember, I don't intend sitting around half the evening, waiting for you to turn up and collect her.'

Even as she spoke, Lauren hated herself. Only one person was suffering from their petty arguing. Zoe.

It was too late to apologise. He was halfway across the car park, splashing through puddles until he reached the Range Rover. Lauren's back stiffened, seeing it parked directly behind her own Mini, where there was no official parking space, completely boxing it in against the wall. If he hadn't arrived to drive away . . .

How a man with no consideration for others can become a doctor, amazes me, she fumed. Then she recalled how he'd mentioned oversleeping and arriving late. *Only for me to beat him to the one and only space.*

The engine roared as he revved it, swinging the Range Rover in a tight half-circle, before shooting out of the gates. Waving at Zoe, Lauren stood, watching the red glow of its tail-lights disappear into the distance, leaving a strange silence around her.

Now it was late, the traffic had eased and Lauren made the journey home swiftly. Empty darkness greeted her as she unlocked the front door, and stepped inside to switch on the light. Only a few weeks before her grandmother would have been there to welcome her, with a hug and a kiss, the smell of the meal she'd cooked filling the warm air of the hallway.

Now, Lauren thought sadly, *that part of my life is over.* So many changes, one after another. First the divorce. Then coming back to live with Gran for those last months of her life. And now the challenge of this new job.

Tugging off her jacket, she hung it up, catching the reflection of her face in the wall mirror. Even that had changed. *Once,* she remembered, *I was pretty. That's why Rick married me, he said. And now, just look at* me.

Through dark eyes, smudged with tiredness, she watched her fingers brush across the sharply etched cheek bones, down past the deep hollows below them, to where her mouth dipped at the corners. A face full of sadness and despair.

Angrily, she glared at the reflected image. *Well,* she decided, *once you've reached rock bottom, you can either give up completely or climb back up again—and there's no way I'm giving up.*

21

The past was behind her now. This job was the new start in life she needed, and she was determined to make a success of it. Stepping into the kitchen, she opened a cupboard, took out a tin of baked beans, tipped them into a saucepan, and began to make toast, wondering what Dr Trevissick and Zoe were eating for their evening meal.

*   *   *

She allowed herself an extra half-hour for the journey the following morning and arrived to find the car park almost empty. Dr Trevissick's distinctive green Range Rover, she noticed, had yet to arrive.

Would he bring Zoe with him? she wondered. She supposed he had no choice. How on earth did he cope with a four-year-old and hospital hours? She knew how overworked doctors were. His life must be constant juggling. How could he give proper attention to either his child, or his job? Work here bore no comparison to the nine-to-five jobs many single parents held down.

There was Zoe's mother, of course. Perhaps she took over when he was on duty. Not that she'd showed up yesterday evening. It must be difficult though, if she had a new family to care for as well.

Poor little scrap, she thought. It wasn't surprising Zoe was so insecure—shunted between parents like that. Lauren wondered how long ago they'd split up, and why. It must be at least a year, judging by the advanced state of her mother's pregnancy. Or maybe that was the reason? Fed up with the unsocial hours her doctor husband worked, she'd found someone else?

Lauren's mind was still fixed on Zoe and her family when she reached the crèche. Being so early, she'd even beaten Sarah, and switched on the kettle so that it would be boiling by the time her colleague arrived.

Helen's remark about Sarah being the reason for Catherine Knolls' departure intrigued her. What could the girl have said, or done, to cause that to happen? Sarah was a bit tactless, but knowing that, surely no one who worked with her would take offence.

And as for Helen herself—she'd made her resentment of Lauren's position quite plain. Lauren had learned from Sarah that Helen and Ms Knolls had worked together many years before. And having worked for the longest time in the crèche, she'd automatically assumed she would become its manager when Catherine Knolls left.

I must have *come as a horrible shock,* Lauren decided.

She was in the little kitchen, pouring boiling water onto the coffee in her mug, when she heard the door open. Guessing it was early-bird Sarah, she took down a second mug and

23

began to fill it.

Small arms flinging themselves round her knees threw her off-balance; the kettle tilted, and sent scalding water across her wrist.

'Zoe!' Dr Trevissick's roar came in unison with Lauren's cry of pain and the child's whimper of dismay. But as Lauren bent to soothe the frightened little girl, she found her elbow gripped by strong fingers and her arm thrust under the running cold tap.

'Forget Zoe!' Dr Trevissick ordered. 'You're the one who needs attention. If we don't see to this quickly, you'll have a very nasty burn.'

'It's all right, Zoe. It wasn't your fault.' Lauren's other hand smoothed the child's hair, trying to comfort her. 'I didn't hear your feet on the carpet.'

The icy water was numbing her wrist, taking away the pain almost before it began. She shivered.

'You're not going to faint, are you?' Dr Trevissick's gaze remained on her wrist when he spoke, but one long leg stretched out sideways, his foot hooking forward a chair. 'You'd better sit down.'

'I'm okay,' she insisted, trying to ease her arm from his grip.

'Which of us is the doctor?'

'But I need to get on. The children will be arriving any second.'

'You'll keep that wrist under the tap until I tell you to stop,' he replied, picking up the second mug of coffee and starting to drink it. 'Where are the rest of your staff?'

'I was in very early.'

She saw the corners of his eyes crinkle above the rim of the mug, and guessed he was smiling.

'To make sure of a space in the car park?' he teased.

Lauren ignored the remark and turned her attention to Zoe, who was watching them with frightened eyes.

'It's all right, sweetheart,' she said. 'I'm quite better now.'

'I didn't mean to hurt you, Lauren,' Zoe whispered, her mouth quivering.

'I know you didn't, Zoe. I should have been more careful when I was holding a hot kettle. Can you unzip your anorak and hang it up?'

As the child slid her arms from the jacket, Lauren noticed that her bright red jumper was inside out, with the label at the front under her chin.

Dr Trevissick noticed it, too. 'Oh, Zoe,' he groaned. 'Didn't you look in the mirror when you were combing your hair?'

'You know it's too high, Daddy, and you said you'd comb my hair. And tie my shoe laces 'cos I can't do bows yet.'

'I don't think your Daddy looked in the mirror to comb his own hair either, Zoe,' Lauren observed dryly.

'He never does comb it,' Zoe confided

25

wickedly. 'His fingers do.'

'You horror!' her father said with a grin. 'Telling tales to teacher.'

'She's not teacher, Daddy,' Zoe protested. 'She's Lauren.'

As the rest of the staff came into the kitchen, their gaze was instantly on Dr Trevissick, leaning against the sink, drinking coffee. Immediately, he bent his head, scrutinising Lauren's wrist, before turning off the still-running tap.

'I think we've caught that in time, but it if begins to cause any discomfort, Lauren, go straight down to Casualty. Tell them I sent you.'

He dried his hands on a paper towel and tossed it into the bin.

'And don't forget—cold running water is the best way to deal with a scald—provided you do it instantly. Bye, Zoe. Bye, Lauren. Be good.'

In a couple of strides he was out of the kitchen and heading towards the door, leaving Lauren to wonder whether it was she or his daughter who was meant to follow his last instruction.

*   *   *

Lauren had made a strong point to her staff about taking a proper lunch hour and having both a meal, and rest, in the hospital canteen. Working in the crèche was exhausting. Small children need constant watching. And with such a variety of ages—the youngest being only four months and the eldest four years—a great deal of care had to be taken to avoid accidents.

Only that morning, a crawling baby discovered one of the three-year-olds threading cotton-reels onto a long lace, and sat fascinated. When the older child grew bored and moved on to play on the slide, the tiny one decided to see what the lace tasted like. Only Sarah's prompt intervention to remove two or three inches of it from the baby's mouth had prevented a disaster.

Needing to set an example herself, Lauren made sure she took a full lunch hour. The canteen meals were good, with plenty of salads.

She was reading a paperback while she ate, deeply involved in its plot, when the chair opposite her scraped across the floor. Balancing a tray with one hand, while he dragged out the chair, was Dr Trevissick.

'Let me see that wrist.' It was a command rather than a request.

Meekly she eased away the cuff of her sweatshirt and stretched out her palm. His fingers drew her hand closer. But the rush of heat that travelled up her arm at his touch had nothing to do with the scalded skin.

'Is it sore?' he asked, studying it carefully.

'Not very.'

27

One eyebrow curved into a question mark. 'How not very?'

'I'm aware of it, but it's not too painful.'

'I don't think it's going to blister, but we'll keep an eye on it. Let me know if it starts to get uncomfortable.'

'Yes, doctor.'

His blue eyes stared deeply into hers. 'Not mocking me, are you?'

'Would I? Now may I have my hand back? I'd like to eat this apple.' She eyed his meal. 'How can you eat all that stodge?'

'Stodge?' he demanded, looking down at his tray. 'Good, wholesome, filling food. Essential on a chilly day like this. What's wrong with it?'

'Well, the vegetable soup is probably okay, but really, Dr Trevissick, you should be the first to know that two fried eggs, three chipolatas, fried bread and chips is the way to a coronary. Let alone a chunk of steamed syrup pudding and custard.'

'I'll soon work that off during the day,' he protested.

'Will you? Rushing about, stressed up—I bet you suffer from indigestion half the time.'

'It's certainly doing me far more good than a plate of rabbit's food,' he retorted. 'I hope that's not what you feed my daughter in your crèche.'

'Your daughter had just had fresh orange juice, two fish fingers, carrots, peas and mashed potato, followed by—I think it was

28

strawberry—yoghurt. She's very keen on fish fingers, Sarah says.'

Dr Trevissick turned down his lower lip wryly. 'She does have them fairly frequently,' he admitted. 'My culinary efforts don't run to exotic cooking.'

'Chicken isn't difficult to roast and you can have it cold for a couple of days after. I'm sure Zoe would like that. Even a sandwich made with wholemeal bread would be better for her than some of the meals she's been telling me about. And most children love fruit yoghurt.'

'Ugh!' Dr Trevissick pulled a face.

'Have you ever tried it?'

'No, and I don't intend to.' He put down his soup spoon and started to slice into one of the eggs. 'You really are a bossy-boots, aren't you? Always telling others what to do. Can't I enjoy my lunch in peace?'

Lauren snapped shut her book and stood up. 'You chose to sit at this table, Dr Trevissick. And don't forget—the creche closes at six o'clock.'

*   *   *

'Thank goodness you're back, Lauren,' Sarah greeted her, with one of the babies tucked into a sling on her back while she carried a second one in her arms. 'Zoe's been going beserk!'

'Why? What's wrong? Has she hurt herself?'

'You weren't around—that's all,' Helen

29

remarked dryly, joining them. 'You really must be very careful or it will become a problem, Ms Mallory. Zoe has to realise you're not here purely for her benefit. If you're going to pull your weight, you can't devote yourself to just one child.'

'Until she settles, I shall do exactly that, Helen. All the other children are perfectly happy, and manageable too, so I don't think it will affect the running of the crèche if I spend a little extra time with Zoe. Where is she?'

'Asleep,' Sarah replied, shifting the baby onto her other hip. 'She cried so much, she made herself sick, then dropped off to sleep on Lucy's lap. They're over there in the corner.'

'You're making a rod for your own back, Ms Mallory,' Helen warned. 'That child must learn not to cling. It won't do her any good in the future.'

Lauren began to understand why Helen hadn't been promoted to creche manager. Her attitude was so wrong. But she didn't have time to argue. All the children had a rest after lunch, and already one or two were waking.

Three mothers arrived to breastfeed and change their infants, an essential part of the bonding process when they saw so little of them during the day. Others were coming off or on duty and collecting or leaving their offspring—something that happened constantly.

Lauren wanted to be nearby when Zoe woke, despite what Helen advised. But she knew the older woman was right when she said that if the child became too attached to her, it could become a problem.

When Zoe did wake, however, Lauren was helping some older children to stick leaves in patterns on pieces of wallpaper. Zoe ran across and climbed onto her lap, her thin arms wrapping tightly round Lauren's neck.

'You went away,' the child accused.

'Only to the canteen for my lunch,' Lauren said, leaning forward to put the top back on the tub of glue.

'You can eat it with me.'

'But you have yours with all the other boys and girls.'

'Want to eat it with you.'

At that moment the box of leaves was grabbed by an inquisitive toddler, who could just see above the edge of the table. In the confusion, with Zoe and several children helping to pick them up, the subject was forgotten.

For now, Lauren thought.

There were enough problems running the crèche already. She wondered whether it were possible to have a second room, or change the layout of this one somehow? With crawling babies and unsteady toddlers vying with energetic three and four-year-olds, it was not only chaotic, but dangerous. Tiny fingers got trodden on. Meticulously built towers of bricks were sent crashing, creating much distress for the budding architect.

Already that day she'd had to ban the children from using the slide when a baby sat on the end and was cannoned into by an older child hurtling down. Divided into those who were actively mobile and those who weren't, life would be safer and easier for all concerned.

With six staff, it ought to be possible. Lauren decided she must explore the surrounding corridor and see if the room next door was available.

As the hours wore on, Lauren became increasingly aware of her scalded wrist. The cuff of her sweatshirt was rubbing the tender skin and she pushed the sleeve up to her elbow, out of the way.

As she did, she remembered Dr Trevissick.

*   *   *

By six-fifteen, she and Zoe were once again the only ones left in the crèche. Seeing the pallor of the child's face, Lauren knew she was tired and anxious, and her anger grew with each passing minute.

I know he's a busy man, she reasoned, *but after yesterday you'd think at least he'd try. For someone whose whole life is dedicated to caring, doesn't* he care *about his own child?*

Her wrist throbbed, reminding her of the concern Dr Trevissick had shown that morning. Why couldn't he show the same feeling for Zoe?

The little girl leaned against Lauren's knees, her small chin cupped in her hands, her huge brown eyes watching the door.

Why doesn't he realise what he's doing to her? Lauren inwardly raged.

Her hand was hovering over the telephone, ready to have him paged again, when the door opened and he was there, swinging his daughter up into his arms as he kissed her.

'I know, I know.' He forestalled Lauren. 'It's nearly six-thirty.' His blue eyes gazed imploringly at her. 'But would could I do? There was a cardiac clinic this afternoon. One of the consultants was called away, so I had to take over. You can't shunt patients in and out at five-minute intervals. Some need coaxing to talk. Others need reassurance.' His wide mouth curved into a smile. 'And some are just long-winded. What else can I say?'

'Sorry?' she suggested.

'On my knees?' he countered. 'Come on, little Zoe. Time to go home.' Locking the door, Lauren fell into step beside them.

'As you can't be sure when you're going to be free, wouldn't it be better for Zoe if her mother collected her each day?' Lauren asked as they passed through the main doors.

Dr Trevissick spun round to face her, the bones of his face sharp in the bright light flooding out from the building.

33

'Zoe has no mother,' he grated harshly. 'I killed her two years ago.'

CHAPTER THREE

Stunned by his words, Lauren stood, not knowing how, or what, to reply. All she could do was stare back at him, bewildered.

Killed her. His voice rang in her ears.

Zoe was holding his hand and twirling herself around, first one way, then the other. 'You'll make yourself dizzy, Zoe,' Lauren warned automatically, feeling her own head spin.

'Home, Daddy.' The child tugged at his arm and he started to walk. Lauren kept pace, needing to know more. But how could she ask? The Range Rover was parked next to her Mini. Dr Trevissick lifted Zoe into her seat and fastened the belt. Standing between the cars, Lauren waited for him to open his door.

When he did, she asked softly, 'What did you mean?'

'Exactly what I said,' he replied tersely. 'I killed my wife.'

'But . . . ' she began, then realised he was still talking in a rapid monotone.

'We were on holiday. The Lake District. Going over one of the passes. I was driving too fast in the thick mist. I saw the headlights of a lorry approaching in the middle of the road, and swerved. We overturned. When the car stopped rolling, Anna was dead.'

'And you?' she whispered.

His voice hardened. 'Me? Oh, I was fine, apart from a fractured ankle. Broken bones mend. Necks rarely do.'

For the second time that day Lauren murmured, 'I'm sorry,' and knew how futile it was. No words yet invented could help.

'And Zoe?' she asked.

His head turned to study the little girl, chattering to a teddy in the back of the car. 'Zoe was at home with my sister. It was only a weekend. A second honeymoon for Anna and me.' He gave a short laugh. 'And I killed her.'

Lauren stretched out her hand and touched his. 'It was an accident, Dr Trevissick. Something no one can prevent.'

His head jerked up, blue eyes blazing at her, full of torment and guilt. 'I was driving too fast in that mist. It was my fault.'

'Or the lorry driver's,' she said quietly.

A deep line drew his brows together. 'The lorry driver's?' he questioned.

'If the lorry hadn't been in the middle of the road at the same time . . .'

'But it was,' he snapped, slamming the car door.

Zoe looked up, startled, from the back seat, then waved to Lauren as the Range Rover backed away.

Starting up the Mini, Lauren felt desolate. *To think I imagined my life was shattered. What torment that man has to live with, constantly blaming himself for the tragedy. How can anyone ever help him?*

There was time to stop at the supermarket on her way home, so Lauren stocked up for several days ahead, carrying four large bags into the house.

I wonder what the Trevissicks are eating tonight, she wondered, rolling out ready-made pastry for a steak pie. *If I made two of these, they could have one for their supper tomorrow. Zoe would probably enjoy it, but what about her father? What was his taste likely to be?*

She remembered the fry-up for his lunch, and evening takeaways. Her mouth twitched into a smile. He'd probably eat anything. Would he mind, though, if she did bring them a meal? He did get quite angry when she'd complained about the meals he was feeding Zoe.

Rick had a temper, too.

Her teeth bit hard into her lip and she glanced down at her arms, expecting to see the purple and green of bruised skin. But all she saw was the redness of her scalded wrist and her mind flicked back to the morning, remembering the firm but gentle grip that had held her arm under the running tap, and the concern that filled Dr Trevissick's blue eyes.

The same eyes that, later, she'd seen

swamped with torment. Something she never once had caught in Rick's eyes.

So alike, yet so unalike.

She wondered what Rick was doing now. Rick and his new wife. Where were they honeymooning? Somewhere exotic? Rick enjoyed basking in hot sun, lying on a beach. Drinking wine. Too much wine.

Her body tensed as she remembered.

His face wasn't handsome then. Skin flushed. Eyes dull. Only one thought in his mind. She tried to shut out the memory, her fingers clenching round the handle of the knife she was using to peel potatoes.

The first time it happened, the fierceness of his lovemaking had excited her. Looking back, it was unbelievable that she could have been so naïve. *Did Rick ever love me? Or was it just that I was there? Adoring. Available. I thought it was love.*

She sliced down hard into the potato, chopping it into tiny bits. *Once I was a stupid little fool, won over by a good-looking face and charming manner. But no man is ever going to treat me like that again. Never, Never. Never.* The knife sliced down, repeatedly punctuating each word, while slivers of potato scattered.

*   *   *

'Shall we start the kids making paper-chains?' Sarah suggested a day or so later as they drank their early-morning coffee. 'Then we can decorate the room and buy a suitable tree. After all, it's only three weeks away.'

Christmas. Lauren hadn't given it a thought. Her time was filled with running the crèche.

'There's a box of tinsel and stuff in a cupboard, but we usually have quite a few home-made decorations that the children do. They love that. Even the tiddlers can stick silver-paper stars on coloured paper for cards.'

'Toddlers, you mean,' Helen corrected.

Sarah grinned. 'Tiddlers is more appropriate for some of them. Potty-training is my biggest hate.'

'Really, Sarah!' Helen snapped. 'There's no need to be coarse.'

'I'm not being coarse,' Sarah protested. 'Just honest. The crèche closes for three days, Lauren—Christmas Eve, Christmas Day and Boxing Day.'

'But what about the parents who work over the Christmas break?'

Sarah shrugged. 'They have to make other arrangements. Most of them take holiday, so they can have the time off. The admin departments are all closed in any case, and there aren't any clinics. It's only the wards that have to carry on, and they send as many patients home as they possibly can.'

Lauren hadn't had a chance to speak to Dr Trevissick since his outburst. He'd brought Zoe to the door and, surprisingly, had been there on the dot of six to collect her again.

The little girl still made a beeline for Lauren on arrival, but was settling down well and mixing with other children. Lauren watched her colouring a nativity scene that Sarah had drawn on stiff paper to make into a card.

'Is that for your daddy?' Lauren asked, bending down beside the table.

Zoe nodded, tongue sticking out as she concentrated.

A scribble of black coloured the head of Joseph. 'That's the daddy,' she explained, and the crayon continued down the rest of the body. 'I'm not colouring the beard 'cos my daddy hasn't got one.'

The baby on the straw was next, carefully outlined in red.

'That's me when I was very little.'

Two wobbly green circles appeared under the baby. 'And my buggy.' Lauren waited, but the picture was pushed to one side.

'Aren't you going to finish colouring it in?' she asked the child gently.

Zoe looked at her with surprised eyes. 'I have finished.'

'What about Mary, Jesus's mummy?'

The paper was dragged back across the table and Zoe studied it with pouting lips. Then, carefully, she picked up a thick black wax crayon and blacked out the figure.

'Just the daddy and the baby,' she declared.

39

'No mummy.'

The matter-of-fact way in which the little girl spoke stung Lauren. To Zoe, there were only two people in a family. A father and a child.

Lauren closed her eyes for a second and swallowed hard. She'd been twelve when her parents finally divorced. An impressionable age. Not an adult. Not a child. But maybe any age was an impressionable one.

The *only dependable character in my life was Gran. Always there when I needed her. And as for my father—another good-looking charmer. The story of my life. I loved him so much. Then he was gone.*

It always happened. Her chin jutted. And the only way to avoid such heartbreak was never to grow close to anyone.

Her hand rested lightly on Zoe's dark hair, and the little girl looked up with a smile. So like her father's, Lauren reflected, with a twist of regret.

*   *   *

When Dr Trevissick arrived to collect his daughter that evening, Lauren was standing beside her. 'What have I done wrong now?' he asked wearily. 'It's only a minute past six— look.'

Lauren gave him a reassuring smile. 'Nothing,' she said. 'But we're starting to prepare things for Christmas and I wondered what you and Zoe will be doing?'

'I haven't given it a thought yet.'

'It is only three weeks' time, Dr Trevissick.'

His eyebrows arched. 'As soon as that? Yes, I suppose it must be.'

'Are you going away?' Lauren asked.

'No, I shall be on duty.'

'And Zoe?'

'I expect my neighbour will have her. Clare, who brings Zoe in when I'm on duty. Zoe always stays there overnight.'

'Isn't her baby due very soon?'

'Around December the twentieth.'

'Won't she have enough to cope with, without worrying about another child? Besides, if it's late, she might be in hospital for Christmas.'

Dr Trevissick's blue eyes clouded. Almost grey, like the sea on a sunless day, Lauren thought.

'I suppose it could happen. Isn't the crèche open over Christmas?'

'We need holidays, too, Dr Trevissick.'

He pulled the hood of Zoe's anorak up around her face and adjusted the zip, then caught her hand in his. When he stood up again, Lauren saw a deep line of worry creased between his thick eyebrows, and felt a pang of guilt for causing it.

'What happened last year?' she asked.

'We spent it with my sister and her family,

41

but they've moved to France now—her husband's job. I suppose I could get Zoe shipped over there.'

'Shipped over there! She's a child, not cargo,' Lauren protested.

She was silent for a moment. This would be her first Christmas completely alone, without her grandmother.

Knowing she was breaking all the rules, she said quickly, 'Would you let Zoe stay with me?'

He glanced across at the little girl who had wandered off and was picking up fallen leaves from a collage on the wall. Then his gaze returned to Lauren and she saw a glimmer of humour in the blue of his eyes.

'From eight-thirty in the morning until six at night?' he queried.

Colour flooded Lauren's cheeks. 'She's welcome to stay for the three days. It seems silly to keep trundling her backwards and forwards.'

'That sounds like a very nice idea. I shall envy her.'

Lauren stared up at him, surprised by the note in his voice. Was it regret? 'You're very welcome to come too,' she began, but he cut in quickly.

'I shall have my Christmas here in the hospital. You'll have enough to do with Zoe around.'

'I'm sure Zoe would very much like you to be there with her, when you are off duty.

Please say yes.'

'Then I'll talk to her when we got home, and see what reaction I get.' He looked at his watch. 'Come on, little one, it's way past six o'clock. We'll be in trouble if we stay any later. Say goodbye to Lauren.'

After they'd gone, his smile still warmed her. Then the realisation of what she'd done swept over Lauren. What on earth must he think of her? Inviting, almost coercing, him to spend Christmas with her! Maybe he had other plans. With those looks, he must have a queue of women to choose from.

*   *   *

Zoe, obviously, was full of approval for the idea and ran in the next day shrieking, 'I'm coming to stay with you for Christmas, Lauren!'

From the doorway, her father smiled and raised his dark eyebrows. There was no need for any other statement.

As the days until Christmas flew by, excitement in the creche increased. And once she reached home each evening, Lauren spent most of her time preparing for it.

She was determined Zoe would have the best Christmas yet. After all, she wouldn't remember those with her mother. She'd been too young. This was going to be one she would remember for ever.

43

The town shops stayed open until late every Thursday during December and Lauren toured them, buying decorations and masses of food.

Rather late, she made a cake and iced it to resemble Father Christmas's face, complete with red hat and twirly beard.

A tree stood, potted, in the shed, ready to be brought indoors at the last minute and decorated. As for presents, she wasn't sure what to do. What was Dr Trevissick buying his daughter? Did he even have time?

Should she offer to help, or would he be offended? Maybe Clare, the pregnant neighbour, would be the one to ask, but Lauren hadn't seen her for several days. She wondered whether the baby, or babies, had arrived.

Helen made no bones about her feelings on the matter.

'You're being most unfair to the other children, Ms Mallory, singling out one for special treatment. In this job there shouldn't be favourites. It's completely unprofessional.' Her long nostrils twitched.

'Do you think I should invite them all home for Christmas then, Helen?'

'In theory, yes.'

'Rubbish!' Lauren retorted. 'Zoe's the only child who won't be spending the day surrounded by family. Haven't you listened to them? Every child is full of which aunty, uncle,

44

cousin, grandma or grandpa they're going to visit, or having to stay. At least Zoe can now join in, even if it is only about me.'

'You're not doing that child any good at all, Ms Mallory. As my mother used to say, "It will all end in tears".'

And probably mine, Lauren thought regretfully, catching one small toddler as he ran past, before he tripped over the end of his trailing sock.

The creche finally closed on the twenty-third at six o'clock. But before it did, the children put on a nativity play for those of their parents who could come. Many who were on duty took their tea break then. The ten minutes it lasted was quite enough, both for the children and staff.

Every child took part, even the babies, who were cherubim with tinsel haloes above their buggies. The most placid was chosen for the crib, two four-year-olds were Joseph and Mary, while the rest were shepherds, wise men and angels. There was quite a surfeit of angels. Zoe was one of them and proved to have a clear voice and good memory, leading the carols.

The children had spent the preceding days helping the staff create costumes, crowns and wings. Lauren felt sorry for all the parents who must have been pestered with requests for bits and pieces of this and that.

On the day, the room was crowded. In the

45

end Sarah left the door open into the corridor so that the overflow could cram its entrance, joined by every passing nurse or visitor.

Lucy and Emma played recorders as accompaniment. The room was darkened apart from one end as a stage, softly lit by lanterns, and the sound of tiny wavering voices soon had the audience dabbing their eyes.

When the placid baby decided to rebel and cry, it produced worried faces among the band of angels surrounding him, until Zoe knelt beside the crib and gave him a kiss. The sparkle of her tinsel halo so fascinated the infant, so that he lay, kicking, clutching her finger for the rest of the performance, evoking ooh and aahs from the whole audience.

Watching the wonder on Zoe's small face as she smiled down at the baby created a lump in Lauren's throat, too, and she felt the burn of tears behind her eyes. If only Zoe's father could see her now.

And looking across the darkened room, she saw him, hands deep in the pockets of his white coat, silhouetted in the doorway. For a moment he stood there, then as the last notes of the carol died away, he was gone.

*   *   *

As Dr Trevissick was off duty until the late night shift on Christmas Eve, Zoe was to arrive in time for tea that afternoon. During the

46

morning, Lauren brought the tree into the lounge and started to decorate it, while she was waiting for some mince pies to cook.

When Lauren was a child living with her grandmother, after her parents' divorce, decorating the tree was a very special occasion. Lots of tinsel and sparkling baubles, along with little gingerbread figures they made together.

The box of glass baubles must still be somewhere in the loft, Lauren decided and, taking up a stepladder, went to find them.

So much clutter, she thought, gazing round at piles of old books, a faded rug, two worn leather suitcases far too heavy ever to use, and several old shoeboxes, some of which were filled with photographs and others with letters and postcards. Her grandmother had always been such a hoarder.

Eventually, having brushed off the cobwebs, Lauren found what she was looking for—an old chocolate box tied with once-red velvet ribbon. Carefully, she carried it back down the ladder.

Unwrapping each one from its crumple of tissue paper, she placed half a dozen spun-glass coloured birds on the table beside the tree. Then, blowing the dust off each one, she hung them on its branches, where the tiny lights created a myriad rainbows glinting.

And suddenly she was a little girl again, kneeling beside her grandmother on that faded rug, watching as each bauble was placed in exactly the right position—knowing that when she came downstairs the following day, a pile of parcels would be waiting.

Would Zoe have the same feeling of magical excitement? she wondered.

For the seventh or eighth time that afternoon, Lauren checked Zoe's bedroom. It wasn't exactly a child's room. Would she mind? The bed was high with a wooden headboard, but Lauren had bought a new flower patterned cover for the single duvet with pillowcases to match, which brightened it up a little. The wallpaper was a pale pink stripe and the curtains a deeper shade of velvet, but the furniture was heavy, dark wood. It was next to Lauren's own room, so that if the little girl called out, she could hear her.

Just after four o'clock, when she was in the kitchen pouring jelly into a rabbit-shaped mould, the doorbell rang. Wiping her hands on a towel, Lauren went into the hall and opened the door.

Dr Trevissick stood on the step, with a rucksack slung over one shoulder and Zoe hopping up and down beside him.

'Are we too early?' His blue eyes looked anxiously into hers. 'You said teatime, but not what time you had your tea.' Lines crinkled upwards from his mouth as he smiled. 'And we didn't dare to be late.'

Zoe was gazing up at the paper garlands decorating the hall, her face glowing with delight. 'We haven't got any shiny ones like those,' she told Lauren, tugging at the zip of her anorak. 'Daddy did hang my paper chains in the dining-room but they didn't reach all the way, did they, Daddy?'

He ducked his head as he came inside and lowered the rucksack to the floor. 'I hope everything's in there,' he said, giving it a doubtful look. 'Zoe helped me pack it, and wanted her entire wardrobe included.'

'Shall we take it upstairs, Zoe? See where you're going to sleep?'

Lauren expected Dr Trevissick to say goodbye, but when he didn't she led the way up the stairs, with him following closely.

'Look, Daddy! There's flowers on my duvet,' the little girl shrieked. 'Lots and lots of flowers. And a really, really grown-up bed, too.' She skipped round the room, examining everything. 'And really, really grown-up curtains. And a grown-up cupboard with dangly golden handles.' She sat on the dressing-table stool and gazed in the mirror. 'My bedroom at home has all baby things, hasn't it, Daddy?' She frowned at her reflection. 'With pink rabbits on. I like these flowers best.'

Her father looked ruefully at Lauren. 'I hadn't thought to change anything. It's the same as when she was born. Anna chose it all.'

His face became more angular when he said his wife's name.

'Will you stay for tea, Dr Trevissick?' Lauren asked quickly. 'Or are you due at the hospital?'

'Not until eight.' He hesitated for a moment. 'And don't you think it's time we dropped the Dr Trevissick bit, Lauren? My name is Matthew.'

CHAPTER FOUR

Lauren repeated the name in her head. *Matthew.* It suited him. She realised he was looking at her intently, one eyebrow raised, in a way she was beginning to recognise.

'I think we can drop the formalities away from work, if that's okay?'

Lauren smiled. 'Of course, Dr Trevissick,' she said, and saw his mouth curve upwards.

Zoe was already leading the way downstairs, eager to discover more about her temporary home. Her mouth widened with pleasure when she opened the door and went into the decorated lounge.

'Shall we make the tea now, Lauren? Daddy's very hungry.'

'Just what I was going to suggest. Do you like mince pies?'

'Do I, Daddy?'

'Probably,' Matthew replied, his gaze travelling the room, taking in the sweet-smelling little tree with its twinkling lights and glittering glass baubles, the holly-wreathed pictures, and mantelpiece hung with swathes of pine and red ribbons. 'Everything looks very festive,' he commented, sinking down into one of the comfortable armchairs.

'You can have a little sleep, Daddy, while Lauren and me's getting tea. Come on, Lauren.'

Matthew threw Lauren a despairing look, which she countered with a grin and, taking Zoe with her, went into the kitchen.

'Right, Zoe,' she said, rapidly undoing plastic containers and setting some large plates on the kitchen table. 'Will you put these mince pies and sausage rolls out for me, while I make the sandwiches?'

Keeping a wary eye on the little girl, she buttered slices of bread and filled some with ham and tomato and the rest with cheese and pickle.

'Do you think Daddy will like these?' Lauren asked.

Engrossed in carefully arranging sausage rolls round the edge of a plate, Zoe nodded. 'My Daddy likes everything. So do I. The sausage has fallen out of this roll. Can I eat it?'

With everything loaded onto a tea trolley—her grandmother had always insisted on using it for visitors—Lauren wheeled it, rattling, along the uneven boards of the hall and into the lounge to find Matthew, head leaning back against the chair, eyes closed. All lines of tension were smoothed away from his forehead, thick dark lashes feathering his eyes, lips slightly parted, his body completely relaxed. Lauren stood in the doorway, gazing across at him, her heartbeat racing.

'Daddy! Wake up! It's teatime!'

Slowly, he yawned, stretching his arms above his head, easing his shoulders, twisting his neck sideways and round, as his eyes opened. Then his wide mouth curved into a smile as he saw the laden tea-trolley.

'After the lecture I had in the canteen the other week, I'm interested to see what you eat at home, Lauren.' He shook his head gravely. 'Remind me to give you a cholesterol test sometime.'

'Well, it is Christmas,' Lauren declared. 'And sausage rolls and mince pies are part of the tradition.'

'Now, little Zoe, from the crumbs around your mouth, you've been sampling already. What do you recommend?'

'Everything! Lauren made it all.'

'Ah, well, it must be good,' Matthew said, and began to fill his plate.

'You have to have a serviette,' Zoe insisted, unfolding one and placing it over his long legs. 'Look, there's Father Christmas and robins and bells and everything on them.' She gave a big sigh. 'I like Christmas. And I really, really like having it in this house with Lauren, don't

52

you, Daddy?'

Matthew didn't reply and Lauren bent her head over the teapot as she poured more into her cup, not wanting to read his expression.

How must he feel, she wondered, seeing his little daughter settling in so happily here? What memories must he have of past Christmases, spent with his wife Anna and their baby? Was he thinking that this is how it might have been, if Anna hadn't died? The three of them, together, in their own home sharing the joy of Christmas?

'May I have a slice of that sponge cake? It looks fantastic.'

Lauren realised that Matthew was speaking to her and quickly cut a slice for him, watching, fascinated, as cream covered his lips, to be licked away with a flick of his pointed tongue.

'Delicious,' he said, somewhat muffled. 'And now, regretfully, I'll have to go. Off to bed when Lauren tells you, Zoe, and no dragging out the time with extra-long stories.'

Zoe pushed out her lower lip and pouted. 'It's not my bedtime yet: Daddy. Not for hours and hours.'

Matthew rose to his feet, his dark head brushing one of the silvery garlands decorating the ceiling, and he stooped to avoid it.

'Don't stand for any fuss, Lauren.' His mouth widening into a grin. 'Not that I think you will.'

Lauren led the way into the hall and watched as Zoe threw her arms round his neck and gave him a kiss.

'Make all the people better for Christmas, Daddy, won't you?'

'I'll try,' he said, kissing the top of her silky hair.

Then, to Lauren's amazement, his hand cupped her own chin, raising her face while his lips brushed her forehead, leaving a trail that blazed her skin. The door opened, letting in a rush of freezing air, then closed swiftly again, and Matthew was gone. Lauren heard his Range Rover roar into life, before it throbbed away into the distance.

It wasn't a kiss, she told herself. *It definitely wasn't a kiss. A mere goodbye-and-thank-you-for-having-me gesture. People do it all the time.*

So why is my whole body feeling as if Matthew had just made passionate love to me?

Zoe was already running back into the lounge to continue her tea, and Lauren slowly followed, her thoughts whirling.

I'm acting like a teenager. What on earth is the matter with me? It wasn't a kiss.

And if it had been, she decided, there'd be a perfectly good reason. After all, she was looking after his daughter for Christmas. No wonder he was thankful. It had taken a load off his mind. He was showing his appreciation. It wasn't a kiss.

A flame of anger flared through her. Men

54

like Rick did that all the time. Why should Matthew be any different?

She began to gather up the plates and cups, piling them onto the tea trolley. Cream and jam daubed Matthew's crumpled serviette. She stared at it, remembering how he'd looked, sitting so relaxed in the armchair, his lean face no longer tense and strained. Something she'd never seen before.

Leaving Zoe doing a jigsaw puzzle she'd found when in the loft, Lauren went to the kitchen to wash up and put the remaining food into containers.

Why didn't I give some to Matthew to take with him? she thought, snapping on the plastic lids. With a long night looming, he'd probably have been glad of them to eat.

She raised her hand to her forehead, recalling the sweep of his lips across her skin, then, annoyed with herself, plunged her fingers into the frothy hot water and began to scour a plate.

*   *   *

'How will Father Christmas know where I am?' Zoe asked as Lauren bathed her later that evening.

Lauren smiled down into the child's worried eyes. 'Father Christmas knows everything,' she soothed. 'He'll know exactly where you are.'

'But how?' Zoe persisted, standing up to be

wrapped in a warm towel and lifted over the side of the bath. 'Who will tell him?'

'The Christmas robin,' Lauren replied, gently drying the little girl's hair. 'Every garden has a robin. Haven't you noticed? And they let Father Christmas know all that's happening.'

'Is that why there's robins on Christmas cards? And your tree?'

'I expect so.' Lauren picked up Zoe's pyjamas from the towel rail, then buttoned her into them.

'Can I have the story about the snowman?' Zoe asked, sliding her feet into her slippers.

'If you hop into bed, I'll read to you, then it's off to sleep before Father Christmas gets here.'

'When's my Daddy coming back?'

Lauren switched on the bedside lamp and pulled back the flowered duvet. 'Tomorrow. He's working at the hospital all night.'

Zoe wriggled down into the covers, her brown eyes troubled. 'You won't go away, will you?'

'Of course I won't, sweetheart. My bedroom's right next to yours.'

'Will you leave my door open in case I have nasty dreams? They sometimes come in the night.' Zoe's fingers were clenching into the fabric of the duvet. 'When my Daddy's not there.'

Lauren stroked the little girl's cheek. 'Of course I will, poppet. And Daddy's not far, only a phone call away. Now, shall we have that story?'

She'd hardly read two pages when the phone rang. Leaving Zoe with the book, Lauren picked up the extension in her bedroom.

The voice was unexpected. Matthew's. He sounded worried.

'Lauren, it's Zoe's presents. I've still got them in the car. I meant to bring them in when she wasn't looking, but with all the excitement, I forgot. By the time I come off duty in the morning, it's going to be too late. She'll be awake by then and devastated if Father Christmas forgets her.'

Lauren lowered her voice in case Zoe could hear. 'It's all right, Matthew. I've made up a stocking for her. Just little things. I wasn't sure . . .'

'That I'd even remember?' Matthew questioned, and she could imagine the hurt expression in his blue eyes. 'You don't have a very high opinion of me, do you, Lauren?'

'Well, you do have a lot on your mind all the time.'

'I suppose I deserve that reply.'

Lauren's brain was already racing ahead. 'Zoe can have her stocking first thing, then we'll have the rest of the presents round the tree later—when you get here. You can slip into the lounge and add yours while I distract her. It won't be difficult. She loves helping me

57

in the kitchen.'

She heard him chuckle. 'I guess she's making the most of it. There's not a lot of preparation with a take-away. I'll have to go. Someone's paging me. Say goodnight to Zoe for me. 'Bye.' The phone clicked into silence.

'Who was that?' the little girl asked, when Lauren returned.

'Your Daddy. He phoned to say goodnight to you.'

'But he didn't,' Zoe protested.

Lauren bit her lip. 'One of the patients wanted him, so he had to go.'

Zoe pouted. 'I want him. I always want him.'

Putting her arm round the child, Lauren sighed. 'I know, sweetheart, but looking after sick people in the hospital is Daddy's job. He'd much rather be here with you, but he has to stay there instead. Now, where were we up to with the snowman story?'

Quickly distracted, Zoe turned to the page and snuggled down again while Lauren continued to read.

'He won't forget, will he?'

'Daddy?' Lauren asked, her mind still on the missing presents.

'No! Father Christmas! He won't forget I'm here, will he?'

'Of course he won't. Look, you've hung your stocking on the end of the bed. When you wake up in the morning, it should be full.'

'Promise?'

'Promise,' Lauren replied. 'Do you want me to leave the light on?'

Zoe wrinkled her nose while she thought. 'Just this little one with the pink hood. That'll stop the nasty dreams coming.' She lifted her head from the pillow for Lauren's kiss, then said, 'You won't shut the door, will you?'

'Wide open, or just a bit closed?'

'Wide, please. And your door, too. Night, night.'

It was nearly midnight before Lauren got to bed, but by the time she did the turkey was wrapped in foil and waiting in the oven, with the timer preset. In all tomorrow's excitement, it would be fatal to forget.

She mentally listed the menu she'd planned for Christmas lunch, hoping it would appeal to both Zoe and her father. Orange and grapefruit slices for starters. The turkey with all its accompaniments. A rich fruit Christmas pudding she'd made herself, and another of ice cream that Zoe might prefer. Mince pies. Assorted cheeses and biscuits and fresh fruit.

Wine was something she wasn't sure about. What would Matthew like? Rick always went for red, but she had no idea of Matthew's taste. She knew so little about him, it was difficult even to try to guess. Taking the advice of the local off-licence, she'd bought two different reds and the same of white wine. Hopefully, one of them would appeal.

And while her brain was puzzling over this,

Lauren remembered Matthew's kiss. She was still remembering it when she finally fell asleep.

*   *   *

Mist hung in shrouds over the hilltops, clinging to the rough escarpments in wisps. The windscreen wipers of the car sliced to and fro, desperately trying to clear the streaming glass.

Momentarily through gathering raindrops, Lauren could see the narrow road, one side close to the towering rock, the other falling away in a tumble of scree. Then it was hidden again as the windscreen blurred.

She could hear the drone of the engine. The rhythmic swish of the wipers. The thud of puddles against the car as it travelled through them.

Beside her, she knew, was Matthew, but all she could see were his hands, white-knuckled fingers clasped round the steering wheel. She tried to turn her head to see his face, reach out to touch his hand, but it was as if her body was stone.

Words strained in her throat, hurting to be released.

The mist was thicker now, like a grey wall in front of them. She felt the car suddenly slow. Heard stones grind under its wheels, spattering.

And then a brilliance of lights blazed, slicing

into her eyes, while the road and the hills and the rocks and the whole world spun.

Her own scream woke her, and she lay in bed, heart pounding, trying to catch her breath. A small pale face was gazing down at her, eyes wide with anxiety. Warm little fingers touched her cheek.

'Don't cry, Lauren,' Zoe whispered. 'I'll stay until your nasty dream's gone away. That's what my Daddy does.'

Touched, Lauren slipped her arm round the child. 'Thank you, poppet.' The vivid horror of the nightmare still clung to her. Was this Matthew's nightmare, too? How his wife had died?

'It's morning-time,' Zoe whispered into her ear. 'There's a bit of sun outside your curtains.'

Lauren leaned sideways to read the clock on her bedside table. Seven forty-five. It couldn't be!

'Merry Christmas, Zoe,' she said, pushing back the duvet and switching on the light, forcing away her dream.

The child beamed a smile, and then let out a shriek. 'Father Christmas! My stocking! Has he been?'

In a tangle of arms and legs, she slid off the bed and out of the door. Lauren pulled on her dressing-gown and, picking up the video camera she'd loaded ready the night before, followed the child.

Zoe was standing, her face white with excitement, staring at the bulging red felt stocking lying on the end of her bed.

'Aren't you going to look inside?' Lauren asked.

'Can I?'

Lauren laughed, directing the camera as she spoke. 'Of course you can.' The stocking was tipped upside down and shaken vigorously, sending a tumble of ribboned packages over the flowered duvet. Carefully, Zoe untied the first one and peeled off the gold paper.

'Crayons! I needed some of those. My other wax ones have all snapped.' The paper came more rapidly off the second parcel, and by the time Zoe reached the last gift, its wrappings were torn off without even looking. Watching her, Lauren wished Matthew was there to see his daughter's happiness. At least she'd caught it all on film for later.

It wasn't difficult to keep Zoe away from the Christmas tree in the lounge. As always, she was Lauren's shadow, insisting on helping with everything.

'I'll do the tablecloth . . . I'll do the mats . . . I'll do the knives and forks and spoons . . . Ooh, I'll do the crackers.'

And all the while, the little girl's excitement and impatience grew. 'When's my Daddy coming?' she repeated every five minutes or so, echoing Lauren's own thoughts. 'Is it time for our special dinner soon?'

'Daddy's got lots to do at the hospital, Zoe,' Lauren told her. 'And we'll eat when he arrives.'

She wondered what kind of night he'd had. The workings of the hospital were still a puzzle to her. As the crèche was her domain, there was no need to get involved in anything outside that.

She didn't even know what status Matthew held. *I really must find out,* she decided, pouring a carton of cream into a bowl and starting to whip it. Fancy working there for all these weeks and not knowing.

'I'll do that for you, Lauren.'

Zoe's small hand closed round the handle of the whisk, and Lauren rapidly had to think of a way to distract her eager little helper.

She was just basting the turkey for its final time, when the doorbell shrilled, making her almost drop the spoon.

'Daddy!' Zoe shrieked, sliding down from the kitchen stool and running into the hall. 'Come and let him in.'

Hoping he wasn't laden with his daughter's presents, Lauren inched open the door, shielding the gap with her body, shivering when she met the frosty air.

'Am I allowed inside? It's freezing out here,' Matthew enquired, the corners of his mouth tilting into a smile.

Before Lauren could reply, Zoe was already tugging back the door to fling her arms round her father's knees. 'Come and see what Father Christmas put in my stocking, Daddy. Lots and lots and lots.'

'First things first, little Zoe,' he said, carefully removing a sprig of mistletoe from the buttonhole of his jacket as he stepped into the hall.

Fascinated, Lauren watched as he held the green-leaved twig over his daughter's dark head, then bent and kissed her.

'Lauren says we must do everything according to tradition on Christmas day, Zoe,' he said, straightening up again, with the mistletoe held high.

'Kiss Lauren, too, then, Daddy,' Zoe instructed.

His head turned and, before Lauren could move away, his lips met hers.

She was aware of a faint trace of spice. That his skin was cold from the outside air. That his mouth was gentle and undemanding. And then it was gone, leaving her with a strange sense of regret.

'Now, come and see all my presents, Daddy. They're upstairs in my bedroom. I had a really, really ginormous stocking and it was filled right to the top, and there was—'

The little girl's voice died away when she reached the top of the stairs and went into her bedroom. Lauren pushed the front door shut. She was surrounded by a feeling of déjà vu— only this time, there was no mistaking that this really had been a kiss.

The turkey was still on the table when she went into the kitchen. Automatically she spooned the juices over it, re-wrapped its foil, and replaced it in the oven, while her mind whirled with a turmoil of thoughts.

Why did I just stand there? Why didn't I move away? He's probably spent the morning with that piece of mistletoe, kissing every nurse in sight. It's the kind of think Rick would do.

But even as she thought it, she knew she was wrong. No matter how great their similarity in looks, Matthew and her ex-husband were as unalike as chalk and cheese.

CHAPTER FIVE

Zoe was back in the kitchen before Lauren realised. 'Daddy said you'd want me to help you some more.'

He was getting her presents in from the car, Lauren remembered. To put round the tree.

'Of course I do, poppet. How about finding the glass dishes for the orange and grapefruit starter? They're in that cupboard. Only be very, very careful how you carry them, won't you?'

Holding her breath, Lauren watched as the little girl crossed the kitchen with each small cut-glass bowl, until the last one was safely on the table.

'I'll do it,' Zoe insisted, dipping a spoon into the basin of fruit.

She was still filling the bowls when Matthew came to join them, one eyebrow lifting in a question mark when he saw her.

'I'm helping Lauren, like you said, Daddy.'

'Can I help as well?'

Zoe shook her head. 'No, Daddy. It's dinner-time now. Lauren and me have got it all ready, so you'd better go and sit down at the table.'

*　　　*　　　*

Sitting on the floor, wearing a red paper crown, Lauren decided she'd eaten, and definitely drunk, far too much. It was easily done on a day like this. Now, as they drank strong dark coffee, it was present-opening time. Zoe was in charge.

The pile of presents had grown to at least five times its original size since the previous night. All Zoe's, smuggled in earlier. Lauren yawned in the warmth of the blazing wood fire and settled her head back against the arm of Matthew's chair.

Through half-closed lashes, she glanced up at him. His thin good-looking face was smiling as he watched his daughter's excitement.

'Just what I really, really wanted. How did Father Christmas know?' she kept repeating, while the heap of torn wrapping paper grew around her.

Matthew suddenly leaned forward as the little girl picked up a flat, oblong, holly-papered box. 'Wait, Zoe. That one's for Lauren.'

Bemused, Lauren took it.

'Just a small thank-you,' he said quietly.

Carefully, she began to untie the red ribbon and the Christmas wrapping fell away to reveal a small, white-framed watercolour. A seascape in delicate hues of blue merging with the pale golden sand of a cove, bordered by cliffs. It was so detailed that Lauren could almost smell the soft salt breeze, hear the crunch of shingle beneath her toes, feel the warmth of the sun.

'I painted it—years ago,' Matthew told her.

'You *painted* it?' Lauren's voice echoed her surprise.

'I spent most of my school holidays near there. My uncle is the local GP and I've a horde of cousins. Well, three to be exact, but they always had loads of friends so it seemed like more.'

Gazing down at the picture, Lauren momentarily had a vision of Matthew as a small boy, shaggy-haired, perched on one of the rocks, his thin brown legs half-hidden in the sea.

'It looks a beautiful place to be,' she said softly.

'It is.'

'I never imagined you were an artist.'

Matthew laughed. Zoe twisted round to see why, gave him a smile, and went back to the book she was colouring with her new crayons.

'An artist?' Matthew's eyes were lost in laughter lines. 'That's something I'll never be. Once, I hoped.' The humour left his face. 'I wasn't good enough.'

'Oh, but you are, Matthew. It's a fantastic picture. So real. It's as though I'm right there.' Lauren turned to look up at him. 'Do you still paint?'

His eyebrows rose. 'When?' he enquired dryly.

'You must have some spare time.'

'Not a second! And anyway, it's just a waste of time.'

'Of course it's not!' Her fingers stroked the edge of the wooden frame. 'Not when you can create something as perfect as this.'

'I'm glad you like it. I didn't know what to give you, but somehow . . . well . . . I hoped you'd like this.'

'I do. Very much.'

A log shifted in the grate, sending a shower of sparks racing up the chimney, and Zoe shot across the room to clamber onto her father's lap.

'Nothing to be scared of, sweetheart,' he murmured, his long fingers stroking her straight dark hair.

Zoe buried her cheek in the thick cream

wool of his Aran sweater and his arm closed round her, his chin resting lightly on top of her head.

The room was growing dark. The only light centred round them from the rise and fall of the flames. *In a little world of our own,* Lauren thought.

Then a little voice piped up. 'When's tea?'

'Zoe!' Matthew roared. 'You must be full to bursting from all the Christmas dinner.'

The little girl sat upright on his lap, shaking her head. 'No, I'm not, Daddy. That was a long time ago.' A smile hovered round her lips. 'And there's jelly shaped like a rabbit and ice cream and a ginormous cake with icing, and crackers, and I'm really, *really* hungry. Shall we make tea, Lauren?'

'Lauren's been busy all day. How about you and me going to make the tea?' Matthew suggested, easing his daughter down onto the floor.

'Yes, let's!'

'But you'll never find where everything is,' Lauren protested weakly.

'I know!' Zoe cried triumphantly, tugging at Matthew's hand. 'Come on, Daddy. I know where everything is 'cos I helped Lauren put it there.'

Lauren scrambled to her feet, but Matthew's hand on her shoulder gently pushed her down into the chair he had just vacated.

'Do as you're told for once, Lauren,' he said

firmly, and let himself be led away into the kitchen.

Settling deep into his chair, Lauren stared into the smouldering embers of the fire, her eyelids heavy. The cushion behind her back was still warm from the heat of his body and a slight hint of spice lingered.

Leaning sideways, she switched on the table lamp beside her and began to study the little watercolour again. It was so detailed. Even limpets on the rocks were visible. Lauren bent her head to look more closely. And tiny clusters of pink thrift clinging to cliff ledges. Tucked away in one corner, almost on the beach, was a grey stone fisherman's cottage.

He'd spent all his childhood holidays there, he'd said. So when did he paint this picture? Surely it wasn't a child's painting? Did he still visit the cove? It was obviously a place he knew well—and loved. She could tell that just by looking at the scene.

Had he taken Anna there? And Zoe?

She closed her eyes, resting her head on the flowered chintz of the chair. He must have been sitting on one of the scattered rocks when he painted it. Or maybe on the sand . . .

Her fingers let the fine grains filter through them, her shoulders edging away from the roughness of the granite behind her back. The waves made a soothing sound, dragging tiny stones with them as they receded, then swished back.

70

Something dug into her spine. Her searching hand touched the spikiness of a limpet shell as she settled her body into a more comfortable position. Matthew was somewhere nearby. Swimming, maybe. Or wandering the tideline. Or sitting on a rock, his long legs lost in the rippling waves.

She knew he was there. Somewhere close. She could smell the warm spiciness of him, mingled with the salt of the sea.

And any second now, she would feel the heat of his eager, tender lips burning over her skin . . .

'It's teatime, Lauren! Teatime!'

Zoe's voice woke her and she opened her eyes to see the little girl dancing in through the open door, clutching an armful of red and green crackers. Matthew rattled along behind her, pushing the tea trolley.

He winked at Zoe. 'You'd better ask Lauren if we've found everything. I'd hate to be in her bad books again.'

*   *   *

Lauren drove back to the crèche after the Christmas break, knowing her life would never be the same again. Knowing that she loved both Matthew and his child.

It was something she couldn't prevent, but didn't want it to be so. Their lives were already too complex. Matthew still loved Anna, and

71

was tormented by the agony of causing her death.

And Zoe? She'd had so much insecurity in her short lifetime.

Helen's right, Lauren reflected sadly. *I shouldn't have brought her home. With me there, plus her father, she's been given a glimpse of how life can be. It wasn't fair of me. I was being selfish.*

But it had been a wonderful Christmas. A traditional family Christmas. Lauren's mouth curved into a smile. Everything a Christmas should be.

Now, life must return to normal. Lauren was manager of the crèche. Zoe, just one of the children she looked after. And Matthew . . .

She stepped out of the car and locked the door. Matthew was merely the parent of one of her charges. There could be nothing more. With a new year ahead of her, she had to make that a resolution. Christmas was over.

Inside the hospital foyer, she met the usual bustle of activity. The lift doors opened. People crushed into it. On the far side, Lauren noticed ruefully, was Helen, tight-lipped and frowning.

Lauren nodded in greeting, but her gaze remained fixed on the closing doors, willing Matthew's tall figure to appear. To see his smile. Smell the warm spice of his skin. Know he was close to her in this confined space.

72

With a judder the lift began to move, and Helen inched nearer, suddenly launching into an attack of words that jarred into Lauren. 'You must do something about getting more room for the crèche, Ms Mallory.'

Lauren blinked in surprise, expecting something quite different. 'Yes, I know, Helen. It's something that's worried me since I took over. Three and four-year-olds can't help being boisterous,' she reasoned, 'but toddlers get swept out of the way and crawling babies trodden on. I've asked the hospital manager for somewhere else in the building—he says it's impossible.'

Helen's long nose twitched. 'You mark my words, Ms Mallory. It'll take an accident before anything gets done.'

'Oh, please don't say that, Helen. I really am at my wit's end to prevent that happening. There has to be some way, but what?'

Dejectedly, Lauren stepped out of the lift with Helen. 'Do you think we've enough time to take down the decorations before the children arrive?'

But when they reached the crèche, Sarah was already there, stuffing armfuls of dusty crepe paper and bits of tinsel into a black bin bag.

'Oh, you angel!' Lauren cried.

'And the kettle's boiling.' Sarah grinned.

Once the children began to arrive, the noise grew. There were new toys to show off.

Exciting events to describe. And routine to be established again.

Lauren didn't see Zoe come in, only knew she was there when two arms flung themselves round her waist in a hug. Quickly, Lauren turned to see Matthew's dark head above the cluster of parents by the door, but before she could catch his eye, he was gone.

Christmas is over, she reminded herself. *Life is back to normal again.*

* * *

There were two new babies that morning, their mothers anxious and tearful when it came to parting from them.

'She needs a lot of cuddling,' one explained, burying the baby's face against her cheek. 'And this is the bunny she holds as she goes to sleep . . .'

'Don't worry.' Lauren smiled reassuringly as she gently eased the child away. 'She'll be fine.'

The second mother sobbed so much, her bewildered little son joined in with a loud roar of unhappiness.

'I'll take him,' Sarah said firmly. 'Come on, sunshine.'

Lauren guided both mothers to the door.

'Come in whenever you want to, or if you're at all worried,' she told them. 'It's not easy, I know, but they'll settle quickly. They all do. It's the mums that take a bit more time.'

74

As the morning went on, Lauren noticed Gina had a streaming cold. The girl sneezed violently every few minutes, continually mopping her nose.

'I think you'd be better off at home,' Lauren advised as the girl dropped yet another paper tissue into the bin.

'I'm fine—really I am.'

'No, you're not, Gina. I do appreciate you coming in, but it isn't fair to the children or the rest of the staff. Now, off you go.'

'But how will you manage?' Gina protested feebly, glancing around.

'We will. I'll contact the agency for a temp.'

But even as Lauren went to the phone, it rang. Jane's mother in Scotland, calling to say her father had suffered a heart attack.

'I must go,' Jane said, fighting back tears. 'Mum sounded frantic.'

'Of course you must. Straight away.'

The agency was doubtful whether they could send anyone that day. So much illness around. Staff holidays going on until the new year. Tomorrow, maybe. Or the day after.

The two new babies were fretful, one refusing her bottle and the other crying non-stop, which soon triggered off some of the others.

Lauren took a deep breath, and jiggling one baby on each hip, tried to encourage a group of older children to do some finger-painting.

'Zoe, you know what to do. Will you show

Fergus and Mandy for me?'

Zoe, intent on her own painting, pushed out her bottom lip and glowered.

'I don't like Fergus. He pinches.'

'Well, if you show him how to finger-paint, he won't be able to pinch at the same time, will he?'

'I will,' Fergus growled, dipping a hand into a pool of brilliant blue and then seizing Zoe's cheek.

Zoe screamed. Fergus shrieked with laughter and spun round to pinch andy's cheek as well. Mandy pinched him back, and all three children screamed, making the babies Lauren was cuddling burst into wails of fright. And through all the noise, Lauren heard an even louder scream.

'Lauren! Quickly!'

Leaving the paint-streaked children, and with a baby still tucked under each arm, she wove her way through darting little bodies to the far side of the room. Eyes wide with horror, Sarah was holding one of the toddlers on her lap while blood dripped down the little face.

For a second, the room wavered around Lauren.

Then she rapped out, 'Ice!'

Tots were gathering round, staring silently at the sobbing two-year-old.

'I think Katy caught her head on the cupboard door. Someone had left it open,'

Sarah gabbled, dabbing at the blood with a tissue.

'Here you are.' Helen thrust a saucer of ice cubes towards Lauren.

'Take these two,' Lauren instructed, passing the babies to her. 'Now, Sarah, let me have Katy.'

With the ice pressed firmly to the sobbing toddler's head, she ran out of the door and down to the lift, pushing her way through waiting people when it arrived.

'Ground floor!' she ordered, and someone quickly pressed the button.

Talking quietly to the little girl, her fingers numb from the ice she held close to the small head, water running down her arm and soaking into her sleeve, she waited until the lift stopped.

Murmurs of sympathy floated behind her as she stepped into the corridor and began to run its length to Casualty.

As she stood, legs shaking, breath tugging in her chest, the doors swinging behind her, a nurse came towards her.

'Someone phoned down to warn us,' she said, taking the child. 'Do you want to come in with her? What's her name?'

'Katy,' Lauren murmured, fighting off another wave of dizziness.

'Hullo, Katy. Now let's see what's happened to you?'

Through a mist of rising darkness, Lauren

heard Matthew's voice. 'A chair, nurse. Quickly! And get her head down.'

'I'm sorry, so sorry,' Lauren murmured. 'It's just that blood . . . '

'Really, Miss Mallory—you of all people, to be squeamish?' His voice was teasing, but when Lauren slowly raised her head, she saw only concern in his eyes.

'All right now?' Weakly, she nodded. 'Sit there, then, while we get this young lady sorted out. A couple of paper stitches and she'll be fine.'

'Oh no!' Lauren cried.

'She'll be as right as ninepence in a couple of minutes. Stay there and don't move. I don't want two of you to cope with. Come on, Katy, my love.'

Once Katy's mother had been found on one of the wards and taken the child home, Lauren's anger kindled.

A phone call later and she was in the hospital manager's office.

'I need extra space,' she demanded, pointing furiously to the stains of Katy's blood on her blouse. 'One accident like that is one too many. Something has to be done. Immediately.'

'And what do you suggest, Ms Mallory?'

'There's a store room next to the crèche. Knocking down part of the adjoining wall would create an extension.'

'If it's a store room, then it's obviously

already in use.'

'For old television sets and other damaged electrical equipment. All items that should be thrown away.'

'I can't just sanction something like that, Ms Mallory. The items would need to be checked by a qualified person.'

Lauren's chin jutted. 'So what's of more importance—a damaged child or a damaged TV?' she snapped, and slammed the door behind her.

*　　　*　　　*

The next morning, as the crèche staff were settling the babies down to sleep, there was a terrific clatter in the corridor outside. Lauren shot through the door to find a couple of men in overalls loading the contents of the store room on to a trolley.

'What's happening?'

'Clearing it.'

'And then what?'

The man shrugged. 'Just told to clear it, that's all.'

Progress at last, Lauren thought happily, until an email arrived later that morning. It sent her, fuming, straight back to the hospital manager's office. He smiled at the sight of her. 'Thought you'd be pleased.'

'Pleased?' she stormed. 'I've just been told to close down the crèche for a week!'

79

'That's correct. We're extending the room, just as you requested yesterday, Ms Mallory.'

'But I can't close it. What about the children? The parents? We've only just returned after the Christmas break. That caused problems for some of them who were on duty. Why can't it be done at the weekend?'

'Look, Ms Mallory, you've been agitating for an extension to your room. Well, now you're getting one.'

'But from today . . . '

'Ms Mallory, consider yourself very lucky to have this extension at all, in the present economic climate.'

Lauren took a deep breath. 'I know. Thank you. But parents just can't arrange for their children to be taken care of elsewhere without any warning. Isn't there somewhere else we could use in the meantime?'

'No, Ms Mallory.'

Her back stiffened. 'And if your nursing staff, auxiliaries, receptionists and doctors just down tools and stop work for a week without any warning, to stay at home and look after their offspring, what will you do?'

His eyes bulged. 'They wouldn't do that.'

'No, I dare say they wouldn't, but some of them are going to be very hard pressed to cope.'

Returning to the crèche she broke the news to the rest of her staff. Their reaction was exactly the same as her own.

'They can't just spring it on us like this!' Sarah protested, peeling off a baby's nappy.

'Well, they have,' Lauren replied, handing her a clean one. 'And we'll have to clear this room before the workmen arrive in any case.'

'Why can't they do it at the weekend?' Emma asked, sponging paint from three toddler's faces and hands while she spoke.

'That would mean overtime,' Lauren explained. 'It'll be a long job, knocking out part of that wall, and rebuilding it into an arch. They'll have to redecorate the whole room afterwards.'

'A week's seems an awfully long time. My dad did our through-lounge in one day,' Emma retorted. 'Will we get paid while we're off work?' She seized a towel and dried the tots' small faces and hands. 'They won't make us take it as holiday, will they?'

'Take what?' Helen asked, bringing another baby for changing.

'Haven't you heard?' Emma said. 'We're closing for a week while they extend this room.'

Helen glared at Lauren. 'Why didn't you warn us earlier?'

'I didn't know myself until half an hour ago, Helen. And if you've any suggestions as to how we can cope, I'll be pleased to hear them.'

'Can't we use somewhere else?' Emma asked.

'Where?' the others chorused.

'The student nurses' lecture room?' asked Emma. 'It's on this floor.'

'What about their lectures?' Lauren reasoned.

'There aren't any until after the Christmas and New Year breaks. My sister's a student nurse.'

'Oh, Emma! You're brilliant!' Lauren cried. 'I'll go and see what I can do.' Fifteen minutes later she was back. 'Anyone prepared to stay on late this evening to move some of the stuff in here down the corridor?'

'You succeeded!' Sarah grinned.

'With a bit of arm-bending.'

'Brilliant! I can manage an extra hour, but then I'm off to see the pantomime. Everybody says it's really great'

'Pantomime?' Lauren mused thoughtfully, her gaze travelling to where Zoe was carefully sticking patterns onto paper. And then she remembered her new year resolution. Zoe was to be treated just like the other children in the crèche.

CHAPTER SIX

The temporary move into the lecture room successfully completed, the rest of the week continued, to the resounding noise of hammers and drills. One or two parents turned

82

up in the wrong place, but soon learned where to go, prompted by a small son or daughter.

Lauren kept a close eye on the building work and was pleased with the result. Even such a small extra area would make a difference to the arrangement of the room, and also give the babies a quieter place to sleep.

At home in the evenings, she spent time drawing plans of where everything would go. The extra door into the corridor from the extension would need a security lock, like the main crèche. Baby kidnapping was a rare happening, but it did happen, and it was far easier to keep a close check on one entrance, than two. With patients, visitors and staff coming and going all day, too many people had access to the corridors of the hospital. No matter how tight the security system, there was always the danger that someone could slip through.

Even though the crèche door had a coded security lock, it was left open for the short times when most parents were delivering and collecting their children. Any other time, they had to ring the bell and wait.

But locking all doors had one main disadvantage. A fire. It was Lauren's biggest fear. Security systems were all very well, until there was an emergency requiring swift evacuation. Fire drill was routine. But in a panic situation, with so many babies and children, what might happen?

'How's the little girl? Katy, wasn't it?' Matthew asked when he came to collect Zoe that evening.

'I phoned her mother this afternoon, and she seems to be fine. Mind your chin, Charlotte,' Lauren replied, as she tugged up the zip on a toddler's anorak. 'I feel so dreadful about it, though.'

'Well, don't, Lauren. These things happen. Especially with a horde of infants racing around. I'm amazed it doesn't occur more frequently.'

'But I'm responsible for each and every child, Matthew. Their mothers put their trust in me.'

Mathew sat on his heels to tie one of Zoe's shoelaces. 'The same thing could happen in their own home. No mother can keep her eye on her child every moment of the day. It's impossible. You really mustn't take this too much to heart, Lauren. No one's blaming you.'

He rose to his feet and tweaked Zoe's hood into place. 'Will you let me take you out to dinner tomorrow?'

The unexpectedness of his question startled her. 'Dinner? Tomorrow?'

'New Year's Eve, Lauren. After all your kindness to us at Christmas, it's the very least I can do.'

'Won't you be on duty?'

He shook his head.

84

'What about Zoe?'

The corners of his mouth tilted. 'She won't be on duty either.'

Lauren smiled back at him. 'You know what I mean.'

'Clare, my neighbour, will have her.'

'The pregnant one? Hasn't she had the baby yet?'

'Another week, she's been told. But she's keeping fairly close to home at the moment. Not seeing the New Year in at some wild party.'

'Thanks, then, that would be lovely. It's ages since I went out for a New Year's meal.'

The last time was with Rick, she remembered. An expensive little Italian restaurant. Secluded tables in alcoves. Candlelight and soft music. A beautiful meal. And at the end of it, he'd told her he was leaving—to marry someone else.

'Lauren!' Matthew's voice sounded puzzled. 'I said, shall I pick you up around eight?'

For a second, she stared blankly at him before his words registered in her brain. 'Yes,' she replied, feeling a pulse of excitement throb through her body. 'Eight o'clock will be fine.'

There wasn't time to dwell on it, though. The working day was beginning. Children arriving. She had to put it out of her mind and concentrate.

It was late in the grey December afternoon when she noticed a haziness near the door into

85

the corridor. Only a few of the children were left. Most had been collected at the end of the five o'clock nursing shift.

At first she thought one of the light bulbs had failed, but even as she looked the haze wavered and twisted. Thickening. Billowing. And as the acrid smell of smoke caught in her throat, she knew she was about to face her dreaded fear. Fire.

Lauren's reflexes took over without conscious thought, sending her running to where the children were clustered, gathering up their paintings to take home. As she ran, with the shriek of smoke detectors deafening her, a fine spray of water cascaded down from the ceiling, soaking her hair, her face, her neck and drenching her clothes.

She could see startled little faces raise, eyes wide with surprise at the deluge. One small boy stamped his feet with glee, splashing water.

Lauren's brain was spinning, trying to remember the fire procedure. It had been so different in their own room. Everyone knew the routine. The children always enjoyed taking part in it. Line up. One behind the other. Quick march. Through the main exit. Along the corridor. Out onto the fire escape stairs. If the corridor is blocked, down the main stairs. Never use the lift. All assemble in front of the building.

It went like clockwork. No panic. No fuss.

But now, in the lecture room, the children were confused, their well-practised routine thrown out of kilter.

Lauren knew there was no way they could reach the main door. She couldn't believe the speed with which the flames were taking hold, flickering along the walls, crackling, gaining power as they consumed every item they met in their path.

Her gaze desperately scanned the long room, seeking the fire escape door, leading out to metal steps. Grabbing Sarah's shoulder, she pointed through the growing smoke.

'Quickly! Follow the usual drill. Count heads as they go.'

Sarah, two sobbing babies tucked under her arms, was already hustling the children towards the door that Helen held open.

'I think Zoe's gone to unpin her collage from the wall,' she shrieked.

Lauren turned back swiftly. Abruptly, the lights went out, leaving the room lit by searing brilliance, sending the terrified children into a frenzy. All Lauren could see were tiny screaming figures, darting towards the fire exit.

Everything seemed to be happening in slow motion. Every one of her senses intensified. The raw throat-biting fumes. Her wet skin cold, yet scorched with heat. Her mouth strangely dry. Her eyes seeing. Her brain comprehending. And yet, it was as though she was distanced from it all, watching a film or a

87

television programme.

The roar of the flames was an unearthly sound. Like nothing she'd ever heard before. And among them, somewhere, was Zoe.

It's the fumes that kill, not the flames. She remembered hearing that said. For a moment, she shut her eyes, trying to blank out the scene, giving herself time to think, quell her panic.

Breathe deeply, she told herself. But it was impossible to breathe at all. *Zoe. I must find her.* Desperately she stepped forward.

A floating spark landed on her jeans and she gazed, fascinated, at the widening patch of scarlet-rimmed blackness, before frantically slapping at it with her hands, quenching its growth.

She couldn't hear the children now. Only the rush and surge of flame. *Zoe.* Ragged pain tore through her. *Matthew's lost a wife. Now, his child. And it's my fault. All my fault. I must find her.*

Every breath was torture.

'Lauren!'

She was sitting on the floor now. How, or why, she didn't know. Somehow, it seemed easier.

Someone was calling. Or she thought someone was calling.

Her tongue slid through dry lips, trying to moisten them, and she opened her mouth to call back, but no sound came.

The effort hurt. She tried again. Nothing.

A beam of light flooded the room, racing towards her, dazzling her aching eyes, and then the sudden force of water burst over her, choking her, knocking her sideways.

'She's over there. By the wall. I'm going in.'

It was a voice she didn't know. A deep voice. A welcome voice. Lauren lay, shivering from the deluge, wanting to open her eyes, but they seemed glued shut.

'It's okay, love. You're okay now. Up you come.'

'No! I . . . must . . . find . . . Zoe . . . '

The words struggled up from somewhere deep in the agony of her throat.

'Don't worry, love. Everything's all right. I've got you safe. Here we go.'

Cold air bit into her, making her shiver. Desperately, she tried to suck it in, fill her straining lungs, but the pain was too much, and she let herself sink down, down into welcoming darkness.

*   *   *

Zoe. She had to find Zoe. Everywhere there was this thick damp mist. She must find her. She must.

'Zoe!' The name was a scream of anguish.

'It's all right, Lauren. Zoe's fine. All the kids are fine. Scared, but all safe. It's you we've been worried about.'

'Matthew?' Lauren peered through the mist filming her sore eyes. 'Drink this. Don't try to talk.'

Something cool and sweet slid down the ache of her throat, and she reached out a hand for more.

'Gently!' Matthew's voice was filled with laughter. 'Just small sips to start with. That throat of yours is raw. And no talking.'

'Tell . . . me . . . what . . . ' Her eyes pleaded with him.

'What happened?'

Slowly she nodded.

'They think it was an electrical fault. Probably the wiring. No warning. Another drink?'

Obediently, Lauren bent her head to sip more liquid.

'Thanks to you acting so quickly, Helen and Sarah got all the kids out and down the fire escape. But then, for some reason, you went back in.'

'Zoe . . . was . . . still . . . Her . . . collage . . . '

Lauren heard Matthew catch his breath, then felt his finger gently smoothe along her cracked lips.

'Oh, Lauren! Sarah said Zoe was first out of the fire exit, tugging all the others through after Helen opened it. All those fire drills were firmly fixed in her mind.' His voice hesitated. 'So that's why you went back into that inferno? Oh, Lauren, what can I say? Zoe must have dashed past you in all the confusion.'

Exhaustion, mingled with relief, swamped over her. Zoe, and the other children, were safe. That was all that mattered. She could still hear Matthew's deep tones as she drifted into sleep.

'The fire brigade was there in minutes. Sarah told them where you'd last been seen. They sent up a platform thing with a searchlight on and . . . If anything had happened to you, Lauren . . .'

His touch smoothed lightly over her hair, and she raised her hand to meet his, feeling his fingers entwine with hers. Then she slept.

*   *   *

It was dark when she woke again. Dark, yet not dark. Light glowed somewhere nearby, and Lauren couldn't work out why it was there. All she had in her bedroom was a central light, and a lamp on the bedside table. But this wasn't either of them.

There were noises too. Strange guttural noises. Almost like—she forced her drowsy mind to concentrate—almost like snoring.

It was snoring.

Wide-awake now, she pushed herself up with one elbow and instantly shut her eyes again as pain shot through her head.

Cautiously, she opened them.

A curtain, patterned with huge yellow

flowers, hung so close she could reach out and touch it. Dimly, on the opposite side of the room, she could see the foot of a bed, metal-edged, its covers humped. Another was next to it. And another.

I'm on a ward, she reasoned. *A hospital ward. But why?*

Her chest felt tight. Every intake of breath difficult. Her skin stung. Her mouth was dry.

And then she remembered. The flames. The heat. The noise. Her fear. Cautiously sliding her feet over the side of the bed onto the cold floor, she stood up, and began to place one foot in front of the other, trying to ignore the pounding in her head and the way the room tilted sideways.

'What d'you think you're doing, Lauren?'

The unexpected voice from behind made her lose her balance, but a firm arm caught and held her before she fell.

'You're supposed to stay in bed,' Matthew growled, and before she could realise what was happening, she was swept up in his arms, his chin prickling her forehead.

Any other time, the indignity of it would have infuriated her, but now Lauren felt far too exhausted to protest. One corner of his white coat lapel tickled her nose and she settled her head in a more comfortable position against his shoulder, feeling his arm tighten round her.

The rhythm of his heartbeat pounded in her

ear, quickening as he bent to lay her on the bed, then was gone as he leaned away. For a second the blue of his eyes held her gaze, yet to Lauren it seemed like an eternity. It was as if she could see into the depths of his soul, read the whole of his lifetime, know his future. His arm stayed, holding her. His mouth so close, she could feel the warmth of his breath caress her skin.

And suddenly, it was Rick's arm. Rick's face. The same fierce strength. The same blue eyes. The same dark hair. Rick.

With one convulsive movement, she twisted her head away, her eyelids closing to shut him out. She sensed Matthew's body stiffen. Felt him step back, his arm sliding away from her, his expression puzzled.

'I'll see you tomorrow, Lauren, and decide when you can be discharged.' There was a bleep from the pager in his top pocket. 'Sorry, have to go. Sleep well, Lauren.'

'Is Dr Trevissick a friend of yours?' the nurse enquired, coming across to tuck in a corner of blanket that trailed on the floor.

Lauren nodded, too weary to explain.

'That explains the privileged treatment, then. Patients usually have to be at death's door to qualify for a night-time visit from the medical staff.'

Lauren yawned. All she wanted to do was sleep. It was as if she was drowning in lethargy, the pillows drawing her in, and her eyelids closed.

CHAPTER SEVEN

Lauren opened her eyes. Someone was asking her a question, loudly and cheerfully. 'Cup of tea? You take sugar?'

She nodded. 'Yes, but no sugar, thank you.' Her throat felt easier.

'Nice cup of tea make you feel better, you see.'

The trolley rattled its way along the ward, and Lauren thought of her grandmother's tea trolley with its embroidered cloth and bone china cups as she sipped the milky liquid.

Swinging her legs out from under the cellular blanket, she lowered them to the floor.

'Did Sister say you could get up?' the girl in the opposite bed asked. 'You can't unless she says so.'

'There's nothing wrong with me.'

With the superior wisdom of one who'd been in the ward for a while, the girl nodded towards the nurses' station. 'They have to decide that.'

'How do I find the Sister?'

The other girl shrugged. 'You don't. You have to wait until the doctors do the ward round. She'll be with them—giving them the low-down on you.'

'When's that?'

'Ten. Eleven. Depends.'

Decisively, Lauren stood up. 'I can't wait until then.'

Even as she spoke the door swung open and, with quickening heartbeat, she saw Matthew stride down the ward.

'Oh, thank goodness you're here!' she called out croakily. 'I need to be discharged immediately. Find out what's happening about the crèche. There'll be chaos, after the fire. I must find another room before all the parents and children arrive.'

'No way, Lauren. We need to assess how much that fire affected you.'

'But I'm perfectly all right, Matthew. I have the crèche to get organised, now the lecture room's been ruined.'

Lauren pushed back the bed cover and tried to sit upright, but a fit of coughing forced her down onto the pillows again.

'Please, Lauren, do as you're told for once. If you're fit enough tomorrow, we'll see. And as for the crèche, that's closed for today. Don't look so horrified. Most of the children need a day to get over their scare, and so do their parents.'

Unable to prevent herself, Lauren slept for most of the day, waking only when different tests were carried out. By evening, she was breathing more easily, and was able to eat some scrambled egg and a slice of bread.

New Year's Eve, she remembered sadly. *When Matthew was taking me out to dinner.*

The patients were settling for the night when he came to see her again.

'I've seen the results of your tests, Lauren, and, on condition that you take things easy for the next three or four days—which means not returning to work—you can be discharged tomorrow afternoon.'

'Not until the afternoon? But there's so much I have to do.'

'I haven't finished, Lauren,' Matthew said quietly. 'Having worked over Christmas, I'm off duty for the next three days. You can stay with Zoe and me. That way, I can keep an eye on you and ensure you rest.'

'But . . . '

'No, buts, Lauren. It's that, or remain in hospital. There's no need to decide, because I've already made the decision for you. Sleep well.'

*   *   *

Matthew arrived soon after lunch the following day, carrying a large plastic bag that he placed on her bed.

'The clothes you had on were only fit for the bin, so I've been shopping,' he said, pulling the curtains round her bed as he backed out. 'I just hope I've got the sizes right. Once you're dressed, we can go.'

Lauren leaned forward and opened the bag, carefully taking out a pale blue polo-necked jumper, a pair of jeans, a lacy white bra and matching pants. But no shoes or tights, she noticed, before delving deeper to produce a pair of slipper socks.

To her surprise, everything fitted, and she stepped out through the curtains to find Matthew sifting on a chair.

His eyes skimmed over her. 'Will they do?' he asked.

She smiled and nodded. 'No shoes, though.'

'Ah, that was intentional. When I said rest, I meant rest.' Gently taking hold of her elbow, he guided her towards the door. 'Zoe can't wait to see you again. I've left her with my neighbour, Clare and her partner. The baby arrived yesterday and Zoe is "helping" Clare look after him.'

'Can I go and check the crèche before we leave?' Lauren asked.

'No.' Matthew's tone was firm. 'The extension is finished, so it'll reopen tomorrow. Your staff can do without you for a few days. They are quite competent, you know.'

The Range Rover was parked by the main door of the hospital and Lauren found herself swept up into Matthew's arms and carried out to it.

'Can't walk outside in slipper socks, can you?' he said, settling her onto the front seat, and tucking a plaid blanket round her.

Lauren closed her eyes. Even the short journey downstairs in the lift had exhausted her. As the engine rumbled into life, she leaned back against the headrest, watching Matthew's hands steer the vehicle out through the exit and into a line of slow-moving traffic.

His head turned slightly. 'Are you cold?' he asked. 'I've turned the heater up high but I didn't think to bring you a jacket.'

'I'm fine,' she murmured, drowsy from the warmth filling the car, and by the time it stopped outside the block of flats where Matthew lived, she was fast asleep.

*   *   *

Zoe was delighted to see her again, after Matthew had collected her from Clare's flat.

'Daddy said you'd swallowed a lot of smoke, Lauren. I did too when all the fire was there. We went right outside and down a *steep, steep* staircase made of metal, so the fire couldn't burn us.' She frowned. 'Some of the children cried. Fergus did. I didn't cry, though. I went down the stairs first when Helen told me to, and all the other children had to follow me. Sarah said I was *really, really* brave.'

'Well, you were, Zoe. Very, very brave.'

The little girl's cheeks dimpled. 'Aunty Clare has a baby now.' She chuckled. 'She's been keeping him in her tummy. He's *really, really* little and has teeny fingers and weeny

98

toes.' Her mouth pouted. 'He cries and cries, too. All squeaky. Aunty Clare says it's 'cos he's hungry and, do you know what, Lauren? She lets him eat her chest.' She paused and looked thoughtful. 'He hasn't any teeth, though.'

'What's his name?' Lauren asked.

Zoe shrugged and raised her eyebrows—just like Matthew did, Lauren noticed with amusement.

'He hasn't got a name. Aunty Clare says she wants to know him a bit better first, before she decides. But Uncle Tom calls him Thingy. That's not a real name, is it?'

'Come on, Zoe. Lauren needs to rest. We'll go and make tea.'

'You're going to sleep in Daddy's bed,' Zoe said, catching hold of her hand. 'I'll show you where.'

Lauren's startled gaze met the laughter in Matthew's eyes. 'Don't look so alarmed, Lauren. I shall be using the sofa-bed in here.' He turned before he went out of the room. 'Oh, and in case you're wondering—it's not going to be fish fingers for tea.'

* * *

At the end of three days, Lauren felt much better. She hadn't realised how devastating the effects of smoke inhalation could be. She also knew that despite the similarity in their looks, Matthew was utterly different from Rick.

Lauren had never met a man so caring. He understood the grief she was still feeling for loss of her grandmother only months before, letting her talk it through, something she'd never been able to do. He held her gently while she wept against his shoulder.

'She brought me up when my parents divorced. They both remarried. Neither of their new partners wanted a difficult teenager. I don't even know where either of them lives. They've never kept in touch.'

Lauren read the horror in Matthew's expression. 'But that's terrible,' he said. 'You mean, they just cast you off, as if you didn't belong to them?'

Her chin jutted. 'I didn't care. I had Gran. She was always there for me. And then I met Rick. He worked at the same pharmaceutical company.' She paused. 'I was twenty when we married.'

'Quite young.'

'Too young. But he was good-looking—and wanted me. At twenty, I thought that was love.'

'And it wasn't?' Matthew asked quietly.

'No. Love is something entirely different. Rick will never understand that. To him, it meant only one thing.'

'How long were you married?'

'Three years.' She gave a wry laugh. 'Long enough to discover what he was really like.'

'Which was?'

Her hands clasped round her wrists,

remembering the bruises she'd needed to hide. 'He drank. A lot. And then . . . '

Matthew's arm slipped round her shoulders, his thumb lightly stroking away their tension.

'There's no need to go on, Lauren. I can guess the rest. Saturday night in Casualty reveals only too well the effects of excessive alcohol.'

'But he always regretted it . . . afterwards. And each time I believed him. You see, I needed so much for him to love me.'

'But you decided to divorce him?'

She shook her head. 'No, he wanted to marry someone else. Listed all my faults. Said I was naive, clinging—a disaster in bed. How she was so different. Then he left.' Lauren's teeth clenched. 'I was unwanted yet again.'

'Oh, Lauren!' Matthew's arm drew her closer, the warmth of his cheek resting against hers. 'Don't ever say that. He was just the wrong man for you. Of course you're wanted. Remember how much your grandmother loved you. And the children in the crèche. They love you so much, Lauren. As for Zoe—well, you already know she totally adores you.'

His eyelashes brushed her skin as he spoke. A butterfly kiss. Lauren remembered Gran calling it that, and she fought back the overpowering impulse to turn her mouth to his, and feel the intensity of his lips on hers.

When it happened, it came as a surprise— Matthew's mouth at first lightly touching hers.

But as her body responded, his arms tightened round her, one hand caressing the nape of her neck, weaving circles of delight.

And the kiss deepened.

Sensations she'd never before experienced, spun and whirled inside her as her fingers slid up into the thickness of his hair, drawing his head closer, and she heard the deep intake of his breath as he groaned.

Reaching sideways, he switched off the table lamp, and a velvety darkness filled the room. Lauren could see streetlights glimmer through the pale outline of the window. Somewhere a baby wailed.

Matthew's heartbeat pulsed in time with hers, the rhythm of it filling her ears. She could feel the slight prickle of stubble on his chin. Taste the wine they'd had at dinner on his lips. Smell the fragrant spice of his skin. Feel the growing warmth of his caressing fingers stroke down her neck, sending a tremor of excitement through every inch of her body.

And then Zoe cried out, her voice filled with terror.

It took over an hour to soothe away the nightmare. Only by tucking the little girl into bed with Lauren could her fear be calmed. And then she slept, while Lauren lay beside her, her own tears wet on her cheeks.

*   *   *

Lauren returned to the crèche the following morning to find everything running smoothly without her.

'It's all down to your organisation,' Sarah said, when she mentioned it. 'We've such a fantastic routine nowadays. Never used to be like this when Catty was in charge. Permanent chaos most of the time. And the extension makes such a difference. You've worked wonders since you came, Lauren.'

By five o'clock, most of the mothers had come off duty and collected their children, leaving only a few. Taking a welcome breathing space, Gina, one of the part-timers, brought Lauren a mug of tea, then sat down on the chair beside her.

'I was wondering if you could advise me, Lauren,' she said hesitantly. Lauren wrapped her hands round the mug, warming them, before she sipped the hot drink.

'If I can,' she answered. 'What do you want to know?'

'It's not that I don't like it here, or anything to do with you taking over, but . . .' She paused, her cheeks flushing. Lauren waited for her to continue.

'What I'd really like to do is work on the children's ward.'

'As a nurse, you mean?'

'Oh no—I'd never be good enough for that.' Gina smiled. 'What I mean is . . . ' She stopped again. 'You see, my sister's little boy—he's only

103

seven—had to come in a while back when he broke his leg badly and needed quite a complicated operation. He'd never been away from home before, so I used to pop up to the ward when I could.'

She bent to tie the shoelaces of a small boy. 'There you are, James—now slip your arms into your anorak. Your mum will be here any minute.'

Once she had the child dressed, she went on. 'You see, they had this hospital play specialist on the ward. She was fantastic. It really helped Stevie. I expect you know the sort of thing they do.'

Lauren shook her head.

'Well, through play, they help prepare a child for whatever operation or treatment they're going to need. They read them stories about hospitals, and let them act out what happens. The kids can dress up as doctors or nurses, too. And sometimes, if the parents can't be with them, they stay with the child before and after the operation.'

Her eyes were full of anxiety when they looked at Lauren. 'It's something I'd love to do. I'd need to take a special diploma course, and as I've already worked in the crèche for over three years, there shouldn't be a problem, but I would need your recommendation.'

Putting down her mug, Lauren studied her thoughtfully. 'You'd have to be very dedicated, Gina. That kind of work, with both the child and parents, must be very stressful and emotionally demanding. Could you do that?'

Gina nodded. 'I'm sure I could. You see, we lost our own little boy when he was three. Leukaemia. So I do know what it's like having a desperately sick child. Everyone at this hospital was so kind then—and with Stevie. I'd like to put something back.'

'I'm so sorry,' Lauren said, knowing how inadequate that word could be. 'I had no idea about your son. But from what I've seen of your work here, in the creche, you're a natural with children. Do you have others of your own?'

Biting her lower lip, Gina shook her head. 'Andrew was our only child, and to be honest, we're just too scared of it happening again to try for another baby yet. Perhaps one day, though.'

'Look, it's getting late now, but I'll certainly recommend you.'

'Oh, thanks, Lauren, I knew you'd help. Helen said you'd try to put me off, because it would mean losing a member of staff, but as I'm only part-time in any case, I'd be prepared to work a full day, one half here in the crèche and the other half on the children's ward.'

'Well, that would fit in really conveniently. See you tomorrow then, Gina.' Exhausted by the end of the working day, Lauren made herself return to the house that evening, even though Matthew wanted her to stay longer.

'Give yourself a bit more time, Lauren, until you're really fit and can cope on your own again.'

Post was scattered on the mat when she opened the front door. Bending down, she picked up a handful of envelopes and glanced at them.

All were addressed to her grandmother, mainly junk mail and some still being sent from different charities, and Lauren wondered just how she was going to prevent them coming.

But one thin envelope was addressed to her. Quickly she slit it open and unfolded the sheet of paper inside, frowning as her eyes skimmed over the heading at the top—it was from a local firm of solicitors.

When she read the contents, her throat tightened.

The house had been rented by her grandmother, but after she died Lauren had continued living there, paying the rent each month. Now this letter told her, in formal terms, that the property, and the one adjoining, was to be sold to a firm of developers for demolition.

She was required to leave within one month.

CHAPTER EIGHT

'Are you feeling all right, Lauren?' Sarah asked, looking closely at her as he handed her a mug of coffee the following morning, before the children arrived. 'Sure you haven't come back to work too soon?'

'I'm fine,' Lauren snapped back, leaving the coffee untasted and hurrying out to unlock the crèche door. 'Shouldn't you be doing something useful?'

Her brain was churning, desperately worrying how she was going to clear the house of all her own and her late grandmother's belongings, in just one month. Having lived through World War II, the old lady had been reluctant to throw anything away. No one did in those days. 'Make do and mend' was the slogan. And her grandmother had kept to it for the rest of her life.

'You look tired,' Matthew commented, when he came to collect Zoe from the crèche that evening. 'Come back and have tea with us.' His mouth tilted into a wry smile. 'I'd suggest stopping to pick up some fish and chips on the way home, but I don't expect you'd approve of that.'

'Whatever,' she sighed, shrugging her shoulders.

His fingers gently lifted her chin and he

looked down into her eyes. 'Hey, this isn't like you, Lauren. What's wrong?'

She picked up her bag and turned to lock the crèche door, fighting back tears. Matthew caught hold of her arm and guided her towards the lift. 'You really do look washed out. Look, why don't you leave your car here, and stay over with us for the night? That would be good, wouldn't it, Zoe?'

Too weary to argue, Lauren let herself be persuaded, and they drove home in the Range Rover, stopping only at the fish and chip shop en route.

Lost in her own thoughts, she sank into an armchair, not listening, while Zoe skipped round, laying the table, chattering away all the time.

'I know which way the forks and knives go now, Lauren. Like this.' She screwed up her face, frowning. 'Daddy hasn't got any serviettes like yours, but we can use kitchen paper. I'll get the roll from the kitchen. Whoops! You nearly tipped that plate all over me, Daddy,' she warned, as he came in.

'Right then, dinner is served,' he said, putting the plates on the table. 'Eat up before it all gets cold.'

Later, after Lauren had read Zoe a story and tucked her into bed, she went back to join Matthew for a cup of coffee.

'Now,' he said, patting the space on the sofa next to him. 'I want to know what's wrong.

You've been very quiet all evening.'

Delving into her handbag, she produced the letter and silently handed it to him, watching his expression change as he read.

'Surely the landlord can't do this?'

'He can. I rang him this morning. The tenancy was in my grandmother's name. I have no right to it. And he intends to sell the property.' She gave Matthew a despairing look. 'You know what an old house it is, with a large garden. Well, a developer has already bought the one next door and made him a very substantial offer, so that he can pull them down and build a block of flats on the site.'

'It's very short notice, Lauren.'

'And dated from the first of January, if you look. That's a week ago, so I've only three weeks left to clear everything, move out, and find somewhere else in the meantime.'

'Well, you can use this flat while we're away.'

'Away?' she repeated bleakly.

'It's a bit of a last-minute arrangement, but my parents are celebrating their fortieth wedding anniversary next month. Their ruby anniversary.' He smiled. 'So my sister—the one who lives in France—has arranged for all the family to meet up. We'll be away for the best part of a month.'

A month! The words filtered into her brain. 'Where's the celebration?'

'Oh, not far from Melbourne.'

'Melbourne?' she echoed.

'Yes. Australia. That's where they live. My father is a consultant at a private hospital there. He's always been rather keen for me to join him, so I'll be interested to see where he works.'

Lauren's coffee cup rattled as she put it back onto the saucer. 'I need to get back home, Matthew. There's so much to do. Can I phone for a taxi?'

'It's late, Lauren. You're tired. Stay over. It won't take me five minutes to put a clean cover on the duvet, and move my bedding onto the sofa in here.' She shook her head.

'Then let me drive you back. Clare will come in and keep an eye on Zoe.'

'That girl has a new baby, Matthew. You can't expect her to be at your beck and call,' Lauren retorted sharply. 'I'll take a taxi.'

And she tried not to read the hurt in his eyes.

*   *   *

The next three weeks passed far too quickly. Easily tired after her ordeal in the fire, Lauren found that, having worked all day in the crèche, coming home to clear out the accumulated clutter of her grandmother's life left her emotionally exhausted. Every item she touched—clothes, pictures, books—held a memory.

110

But it had to be done—and quickly, too. There wasn't time to linger over treasured possessions. Everything had to go.

In between, she was sifting through estate agents' details and visiting those that sounded a possibility. But it didn't take her long to realise that what was written on paper bore very little resemblance to what she actually found on inspection. Flats she really liked were out of her price range, and those she could afford were dreadful.

Matthew came with her on the rare occasions when he wasn't on duty, and without him she would never have noticed small imperfections like a damp patch under a rusting radiator, sash windows held by frayed cords, or the dark stain of mould hidden behind a wardrobe. But by the end of the month, when she had to move out, she knew she would be homeless. To make things worse, Matthew and Zoe left for Australia the day before then.

While she was in the crèche, Zoe had been drawing or painting complicated pictures of aeroplanes and kangaroos, with an occasional monkey dangling from a tree.

'There won't be any monkeys, Zoe,' Lauren told her, eyeing the latest work of art.

'There might be,' the little girl insisted. 'One could escape from that zoo where Daddy took me, and hop onto a plane when nobody was looking, and hide under someone's seat,

111

then hop off when the plane landed.'

'Yes,' Lauren agreed. 'It could, but I think someone might notice.'

'Not if it hid in a buggy. Then everyone would think it was a baby.' Lauren gave in. At times, Zoe's logic defeated her.

The day before they left for Australia, Matthew gave her the keys and moved what remained of her belongings into his flat.

'Please still be here when we get back, Lauren,' he said, his eyes looking deep into hers.

It was strange being there without him and Zoe, too. So quiet, apart from the occasional wail of Clare's baby next door. In the darkness, sleeping in his bed, Lauren could smell the faint spice of his aftershave, remembering the warmth of his cheek against hers, the slight prickle of stubble on his chin, the brush of his eyelashes over her forehead, and the way he'd kissed her—just that once.

It was a kiss she would never forget, nor the depth of feeling it had aroused in her. Something Rick had never done.

Why do I have to keep remembering him? she wondered. Matthew could never be like Rick.

*   *   *

A day or two later, while searching through his bookshelves, trying to find something to read, she pulled out a folder tucked into a book on the West Country. Inside was a collection of small paintings, all delicate watercolours of the sea and a sandy beach. Looking more closely, she recognised it as the cove in the painting Matthew had given her for Christmas.

So this must be where he'd spent his holidays as a child, she thought, her fingertip lightly smoothing the surface of the paper. Each painting was so detailed and beautiful that she could almost imagine herself stepping onto the soft sand, and feeling the warmth of tiny waves caressing her feet.

The book lay open on the floor beside her. Picking it up, she glanced at the page of old black and white photographs. Photographs of the same cove. A place very special to Matthew.

And suddenly, she wanted to be there. See it for herself. Know the peace and tranquillity it held. And the magic that had captivated him so much, that he kept painting it.

*   *   *

'There's someone downstairs asking for you, Lauren,' Sarah told her, as she came into the kitchen for a mug of tea, while the children were having their rest after lunch the next day. 'One of the receptionists just rang.'

'Did they give a name?'

'She didn't say.'

'Okay then, I'll try not to be too long. It's

probably a prospective parent wanting details of the crèche.'

As the lift doors sighed open on the ground floor, she stepped out, her eyes searching for whoever was waiting.

'Hullo, darling.'

Her body turning to ice, she spun round to find Rick standing behind her. Then she was caught in his arms as he pulled her towards him, his mouth closing over hers.

Frantically, she twisted her head sideways, trying to pull away, shuddering as his wet lips slid across her cheek, but his grip tightened.

'What a job I've had to find you,' he murmured into her ear, and she could smell the alcohol on his breath. 'Let's go and sit down over there, shall we, darling?'

'What are you doing here?' she hissed, sinking onto the edge of a chair, before her trembling legs gave way. 'How did you know where I was?'

'It wasn't easy, I can tell you, especially when I saw the Sold sign outside your grandmother's house. One of your neighbours said you worked at the hospital, so here I am.'

'But why?'

'I want you back.'

'What?' Several heads turned as her voice rose.

He laughed, and Lauren noticed a roll of fat that quivered under his chin. marring its perfection. 'I guessed that would surprise you.'

114

'And what does your new wife have to say about that?'

'Let's forget about her, shall we, darling? An aggressive little creature she's turned out to be.'

'You mean, she fights back? Not like me?'

A flush reddened his cheeks. 'I said, forget about her. It's you I want. Never should have let you go.' He rose unsteadily to his feet. 'So, what time do you finish here? I'll be waiting.'

Looking at him, Lauren felt a sudden rush of revulsion, and wondered why she'd ever been attracted to him. Was it his looks? Or just that she needed to feel secure? Now she knew the real person, any love she once had for him was long gone. She'd grown up, gained confidence, and met a man so different in every way. Now, she knew what love really meant.

'There's no way I'm coming back to you, Rick. No way at all.'

His fingers gripped her wrist, nails biting into her skin. 'I'll be waiting for you, Lauren. Outside. Tonight. Don't forget."

She refused to let him see her fear, making herself meet his eyes, trying to stop her body from shaking. 'I have to get back to work,' she said, hardly recognising her own voice, and felt his grip fall away.

Head held high, back straight, she controlled her footsteps as she walked back to the lift, seeing the doors open and a group of

115

chattering nurses come out. But once inside, her body shook and tears scalded her cheeks.

*　　　*　　　*

'Really, Ms Mallory,' Helen chided, later that afternoon. 'You're putting Charlotte's anorak on Fergus, and they're both wearing someone else's shoes. I do think you've returned to work far too soon. What with the fire, and having to move out of your home, it's obviously been very traumatic for you. Why don't you take some time off?'

'Yes, Helen, I think I will,' Lauren replied, standing up and handing the anorak to her. 'You all managed perfectly well without me when I was away, so I'm sure there'll be no problems if I do so again. Here are the keys.'

The amazement on Helen's face was the last thing she saw, as she walked out and closed the door.

Terrified that Rick was already waiting for her, she ran down the back stairs and out through a side exit to reach the car park, constantly glancing behind. Her car was parked next to the main gates and once inside it, she started the engine and drove through them at high speed, narrowly missing a van in the road outside.

Back in Matthew's flat, she finally felt safe again. There was no way Rick would find her there.

Rain was pattering against the window. Lauren got up and drew the curtains, shutting out the night, then went into the kitchen to open a tin of baked beans and put bread into the toaster. *Matthew might not think so, but it's a really healthy meal,* she thought.

Matthew. Today was the ruby wedding celebration. Zoe would be in her element. Meeting her grandparents and all her aunts and uncles. Being thoroughly spoilt. And why not?

She wondered what Matthew was doing—and whether he was thinking of her. Or, being in the company of his family again, was she completely forgotten? Just someone who worked at the hospital, like he did. Nothing more. Why did that thought hurt so much?

CHAPTER NINE

It was dark when Lauren woke the next morning. Rain still pattered at the windows and she could hear Clare's baby wailing in the flat next door. For a moment or two, she lay, deep in the warmth of Matthew's duvet, wondering how she would fill her day, when the phone by the bed rang.

A surge of delight winged through her. It would be Matthew. Wanting to tell her about the ruby wedding celebrations. Quickly, she picked it up, eager to hear his voice.

'I want you back, Lauren.'

Horrified, she let the phone fall from her hand onto the pillow, questions pulsing through her brain. Who in the crèche had given Rick this number? Did he have the address, too? Was he already on his way? Where could she go that no one else knew about? Where she would be safe from him?

As she pushed back the duvet, the book on the West Country fell to the floor, and lay there, open.

Matthew's cove!

Within ten minutes she'd found a road atlas, packed a small bag, left a note for Matthew, and in a state of panic was driving towards the motorway.

By afternoon she'd reached Bodmin Moor, where thin mist drifted across the road, blotting it out every now and then. Soon it would be dark. But no way could she go back. Not if Rick was there, waiting. She had to find Matthew's cove. There would be hotels or guest houses nearby where she could stay. Pulling into a lay-by, she peered anxiously at the map to see how much further she had to go.

It was nearly four o'clock before she passed Helston, and after the Air Sea Rescue base at Culdrose, the road twisted and turned for several miles, getting narrower, finally turning into a single-track lane.

At last she could hear, and smell, the sea as the track ended in shingle, but it was far too dark for Lauren to see anything at all. Dank air enveloped her as she stepped stiffly out of the car and began to shiver.

The crunch of footsteps made her swing round, startled. An elderly man, face almost buried in the hood of his thick anorak, stood, staring at her in the darkness, a small dog close by his side.

'Lost your way, have you, my dear? 'Tis a dead-end here.'

'Yes,' she said, her voice quivering with tiredness and despair. 'I've come on such a long journey and now I don't really know where I'm going.'

'Where be you staying?'

'Nowhere.'

'Nowhere?' His voice was quite incredulous. 'No hotel, nor nothing?'

She shook her head. 'I just wanted to be here. But now . . . '

'Then you come along with me, my dear. Rose, my wife, and I will take you in for the night. Young maid, like you. Nowhere to stay.' He shook his head in disbelief. 'I'll walk on ahead,' he said, pointing a hand. 'Where those lights are. That be our cottage. ' 'Tisn't far.'

*   *   *

Later, surrounded by warmth and kindness,

while the old couple fussed round, bringing home-made soup and thick slices of granary bread, Lauren couldn't stop tears from sliding down her cheeks.

'Now, my dear, don't you take on so. Tired out, you'll be. Long journey and then finding nowhere to stay,' Rose comforted. 'Eat up that soup, afore it gets cold. Don't reckon you've had much all day, have you? Ted and me've made up the bed in our spare room.' She patted Lauren's hand. 'Come morning, things won't seem so bad, you'll see.'

Lauren found her eyelids drooping before she'd even finished the soup and let herself be led up a narrow flight of wooden stairs into a room almost filled by a high double bed. Through the tiny diamond-paned window, she could see stars glitter in the frosty sky and hear the soft swish of waves.

And then she slept.

*　　　*　　　*

A tapping on the door woke her as Rose popped her head round. 'Sleep well, my dear?' she asked, carrying in a pretty china cup of tea. 'Bit brighter this morning, though my Ted says there was a frost early on. I've put out a towel for you in the bathroom. Take your time, my dear. There'll be bacon and eggs when you be ready. Keep a few hens, I do, so they be new laid.'

When she'd gone, Lauren pulled back a corner of the sun-faded curtain and looked out through the salt-hazed glass. Her mouth curved with delight.

Below the cottage, only metres away, tiny waves swirled in along the edge of the shoreline, pushing strands of seaweed across the sand, exactly as in the watercolour Matthew had given her for Christmas.

She'd found it. The same view. And she was sleeping in the same little fisherman's cottage he'd painted all those years ago!

After she'd bathed and dressed, she joined Rose in the kitchen.

'Porridge be all right for you, my dear?' Rose asked. ''Tis what we do have, winter-time. Bacon comes from farm over the hill, so 'tis always good.' She chuckled. 'Could choose your own pig, if you wanted, I reckon.'

'Have you always lived here, Rose?' Lauren asked, when she'd finished breakfast and was still sitting at the table, drinking more tea.

'In this cottage?' Rose said, brushing toast crumbs from the cloth, and nodded. 'Since we wed, and that's nigh on fifty years. Not that I'm complaining. My Ted's a good man.'

'Did a doctor and his children live nearby? About twenty years ago?

Rose laughed. 'You mean Doctor Zennor? He's still doctor here. Though he's away now. At his sister's over in Australia for some celebration, I've heard tell.'

Leaning back in her chair, Lauren studied the view through the window, already knowing every tiny detail from the perfection of Matthew's painting.

'Were you thinking of staying down here long?' Rose asked.

'I'd like to.' Lauren hesitated, before continuing. 'You see, I was caught up in a fire a while back, and it's taking a bit longer than I realised to feel really fit again.' She let her gaze return to the peaceful view. 'And I thought here . . . ' Her voice trailed away.

'Ah, my dear, 'tis a restful place. And, should you want to, you're welcome to stay as long as you like. My Ted and me'd be only too pleased for your company.'

Overwhelmed by such kindness, Lauren said yes. Having lived with her grandmother for a large part of her life, she found it easy to get on with Rose, and the older woman was delighted to take Lauren under her wing.

'Ted and me never were blessed with children,' she confided one afternoon as they were making scones for tea. 'Grieved me more'n him, I reckon. Still, my four sisters made up for that with ten between them. Always had one or t'other's children around here. Doctor Zennor's youngsters used to come along with them. Liked my scones, they did.'

Thumping a lump of dough onto a wooden board, she began to knead it with deft hands. 'I remember one little lad. Came down summer-times. Always drawing, he was. Out there, sitting on a rock.' She inclined her head towards the living room. 'Gave me that painting in there, when he were a bit older. To thank me for all them scones, he said.'

Lauren got up and went to look at a delicate watercolour of the cove, showing Rose and Ted's cottage. It was so similar to her own that Lauren knew it had to have been painted by Matthew.

'Can you remember his name, Rose?'

'Oh, my dear, 'tis long ago now, and there were so many of them children. Dark hair, he had. That I do remember.' She pursed her lips as she thought. 'Mark, or were it Martin?'

'Matthew?' Lauren prompted.

'Matthew! That's right, my dear. Not one of they Zennor children though. Cousin, I think he might have been.' Her hands were swiftly shaping the dough into rounds as she spoke.

Lauren spent each day wandering along the beach, or climbing up and along wind-swept cliff paths, spray rising in the air to softly dampen her face and hair. The gentle peace surrounding her was a balm, soothing away all the unhappiness of recent years.

Sometimes Ted or Rose walked with her, recounting tales of times long past, when tin mines flourished, and smugglers used the cove. And once Ted took her with him in his boat to catch mackerel that they brought home and

Rose grilled for their dinner.

At night she slept deeply, the sound of waves and drag of shingle as they swept back and forth along the shore, hypnotic in their rhythm. Sinking down under thick blankets, she could gaze across to the window where a myriad stars glittered in the frosty sky. But she knew there was something she had to do before she could truly find the peace she wanted so much.

*   *   *

'I have to leave you for a while,' she said one evening as they ate steaming pasties, freshly made by Rose.

'Leave us? Oh, my dear.' Rose's face crumpled.

'Only for a day or two. I promise I'll be back. It's just that . . . ' Lauren's voice died away, knowing she couldn't explain.

The journey seemed to take forever, or maybe it was because of her reluctance to do it. But, finally, late in the afternoon, she parked the car outside Matthew's flat and went inside.

Her note was as she'd left it, propped up against the telephone in the hall, where he'd see it as soon as he returned. Lauren moved it to one side while she dialled a number.

'Rick? I need to see you.'

They were to meet in a pub several miles

away from Matthew's flat. Neutral ground. Trying unsuccessfully to stop her body from trembling, Lauren pushed open the swing door, hearing a burst of voices and laughter, feeling the sudden heat after the chill outside.

Her gaze moved to the bar, seeing the back of Rick's head, his dark hair expertly cut, the straight line of his shoulders in their black leather jacket, the glass in his hand. As if sensing her presence, his head turned. But it wasn't Matthew's lookalike she saw any more. How could she ever have thought them so similar? Rick's features were no longer clear-cut, his cheeks reddened, mouth drooping.

Straightening her back, she stepped towards him.

'Darling!' he slurred. 'Knew you'd come back. What are you drinking?'

Lauren shook her head. 'I just want to talk. There's a table over there.' She felt his hand rest on her hip as they crossed the other side of the room, and sat down facing him.

'I want you to understand, Rick, that I'm never coming back to you. My whole life is different now. And you will never be part of it.'

His fingers shot across the table to clasp round her wrist, nails biting into her skin, something she remembered too well. But suddenly the strength of her own hand caught the back of his, lifting it away with surprising ease, and she made herself look straight into his eyes.

Once those eyes, and his strength, had been a power to hold her. Keep her as his possession. But now they no longer controlled her.

'Go back to your new wife, Rick,' she said, rising to her feet. 'I never, ever want to see, or hear from you again because, if I do, then the police will be told exactly what you did to me.'

'You wouldn't . . . '

'I would.'

She turned, head held high, and walked away from him, out through the door into the frosty night, ready for her long drive back to Matthew's cove.

CHAPTER TEN

Lauren went down the narrow wooden staircase, suddenly feeling very happy. Sunshine filtered in through every salt-hazed window, creating a myriad dazzling rainbows where it touched the tiny sails of a glass galleon on the shelf above the fireplace. From outside came the soft swish of waves along the shore. Spring always came early to Cornwall and, on a day like today, she was sure it had already begun.

Later that morning sitting in Rose's little kitchen, spreading clotted cream and strawberry jam over a hot scone as they chatted together, she heard the sound of a vehicle coming down the track.

A car door slammed and Rose got up to see who it was. Voices echoed. One high. One deep. Lauren's breath caught in her throat. Then, she too was on her feet, running across the room, as Matthew and Zoe came in.

Rose chuckled. 'What did I tell you, my dear? Always appeared, this one did, just as my scones were on the table.'

With Zoe clinging to her like a limpet, and Matthew gazing at her in amazement, Lauren didn't know who to speak to first.

'You found my note,' she said.

'Note?' Matthew raised one eyebrow in a way Lauren had grown to love. 'No, we haven't been back to the flat yet. My uncle sprained his ankle falling down the plane steps at the airport, so I've driven him home. And Zoe's heard so much about Rose's scones, she asked to see her while we were here.' He hugged his daughter. 'But what are you doing here, Lauren?'

'It's a long story,' she said slowly. 'So enjoy your scone first, and then I'll tell you.' She waited until Zoe had joined Rose in the kitchen to help make a cake for tea, before doing so.

'You're never going back to him?' Matthew asked, when she'd finished.

'Never. Rick has no power over me any more.'

Matthew's long fingers lightly swept her cheek. 'I needed to know that.' Pushing back his chair, he stood up. 'There's something I have to tell you, Lauren—I've been offered a new job.'

Her body tensed. This was what she'd been dreading ever since Matthew left for Australia, remembering his words: *My father's a consultant at a private hospital there. He's always been rather keen for me to join him.*

She heard his voice continue. 'While Zoe's absorbed with her cake-making, shall we walk along the beach?'

Strands of seaweed, abandoned by the tide, clung to the shoreline where wading birds delved into the wet sand, rising in a flurry of wings as they passed. Wanting to delay hearing what he had to tell her, Lauren stopped by a cluster of rocks. 'Is this where you painted my watercolour?'

His eyes crinkled as he smiled. 'It was my favourite spot. I was always painting this view. It's never the same two days running, constantly changed by the wind, or light, or tide. I'd almost forgotten how amazing it is.' Slipping his arm round her shoulders, he turned her towards him. 'Lauren, about this new job—while we were in Australia . . . '

'Oh, look!' She interrupted him, bending under his arm to gaze down into one of the deep rock pools. 'See. A baby crab. And there. I think it's a starfish. We should have brought

Zoe with us, Matthew. She'd love finding all these sea creatures.'

'Lauren, listen to me, please. This is important.'

Reluctantly, she met his gaze, not wanting to hear what he would say.

'When we were in Australia my uncle and I had a serious talk. I probably told you that he's the doctor here, in Cornwall. Well, now he wants to retire.' Matthew tilted her chin and looked down into her eyes.

'None of his children has gone in for medicine, so he's asked me to take over his practice as GP. It would mean leaving the hospital, but life would be so different living here, Lauren—especially for Zoe.' He paused. 'And I want you to come with us.'

Running his hand through his tousled hair, he continued in a rush of words. 'I missed you so much while I was away, and I know I can't live my life without you there, too.' He shook his head impatiently. 'Oh, this is hopeless. What I'm trying to say, Lauren, is that I love you. I have done ever since I met you in the hospital car park that morning. Will you marry me?'

'Yes, Matthew.'

He stared blankly at her for a long moment. 'Did you say yes?'

She laughed, reaching up to pull him closer, his lips tasting of strawberry jam and cream as their mouths met.

'Lauren! Daddy! Come and see.' Zoe was jumping up and down in the cottage doorway. 'Me and Rose have made a *really, really* ginormous cake and Rose says I can put the icing on it later. Can I stay for a while?'

Wiping her floury hands on her apron, Rose chuckled. 'Quite a little chatterbox, is your Zoe.' Her gaze darted from one to the other. 'Now I can see you'm a lot to talk about, so off you two go. And don't be worrying about this little maid. She'll be fine along with me.'

Matthew caught hold of Lauren's hand, tugging her across the sand. 'If we go up over the cliffs, the path takes us right down to my uncle's house. His surgery is there, too, but a new medical complex is almost completed nearer to Penzance, so it'll be moved into that.'

He stopped to lift a strand of windswept hair away from her eyes. 'Would you mind very much not going back to the crèche? You've done so much for it since you started there.'

Slipping her arms up to link her fingers behind his neck, she moved closer to him, gazing back into the deep blue of his eyes. 'Wherever you are. that's where I want to be, Matthew. With you and Zoe. Nothing else matters. And as for the crèche, they've managed so well without me, I doubt they'll even notice.' Her cheeks dimpled as she smiled. 'Anyway, this new medical complex— won't it need a crèche as well?'

They strolled along in silence for a while, fingers intertwined, but Lauren knew she had one more question to ask.

'Anna,' she said, turning to him. 'And the guilt you feel over her death.'

'You took that guilt away from me, Lauren. Remember? When you spoke about the lorry being driven in the middle of the road. You were right. It was that driver's guilt, not mine. I'd never thought about it in that way.'

'And your love for her?'

'I did love Anna, and always will, but that was a different love for a different woman. Now,' he said, drawing her into his arms. 'It's you I love.' And she was lost in the depths of his kiss.

'We must tell Zoe,' Lauren insisted, as they went back to the cottage. 'D'you think she'll mind sharing her Daddy with me?'

But she needn't have worried. On hearing the news as the three of them walked over the sand, the little girl slipped her hands into theirs, saying, 'Now I'll have a Daddy and a Mummy, and we'll really, really be a family.'

A family, Lauren thought contentedly.

Lauren and Zoe stayed on with Rose and Ted, while Matthew returned to clear his flat and work out a month's notice at the hospital. Each weekend he joined them, and together they found another cottage near the cove.

Spring filled the hedgerows with primroses and violets, and later the woods were hazed in bluebells. Their wedding, in a tiny grey-stone church, was to be a quiet one. Ted, proud to give Lauren away. Zoe, the bridesmaid in a fairytale dress.

Waking that morning, seeing the cove under a sky of blue brilliance patterned with tiny white clouds, Lauren had only one thought in her mind. *Today I'm getting married again, but this time it will be for ever.*